Cry Wolf

a psychological thriller

To Eric, my friend who helps everyone,

Julie

by Julie Davey

ISBN 10 1468035274
ISBN 13 9781468035278

Cry Wolf: a psychological thriller

Cover image "*Howler*" by Shannon Johnson.

In memory of Dr. Lois Neil Sambar,
my dear friend and colleague

Acknowledgements

My husband, Bob, my one-member fan club, is always cheering me on and encouraging me to write. Without his support, confidence and understanding, I would not have attempted this project.

Since the story was inspired by actual events, I would especially like to thank Dorothy Maloney Woltemath who was with me when my parents took us to the remote mountain cabin in which an eccentric couple they had befriended lived with a dozen wolves. Without her eyewitness backup about the highly unlikely foundation for this novel, I probably would never have written it. It would have seemed too "over the top." Also, Dorothy was editor of our high-school newspaper in Colorado Springs and coerced me into joining its staff, a decision that pointed me in the direction of writing and teaching, both of which have become my life's work. She also edited and improved the *Cry Wolf* manuscript.

Laura Seiler also read and edited the manuscript several times over the years and did its final edit. In addition, Bill Durkee, who edited my 2007 *Writing for Wellness* book, provided significant review of this one. Also reading the manuscript and providing suggestions on it and the cover were Markie Ramirez, Marna LeBeck, Lynda Koehler, Joan Smith, Karen Gilbert, Linda Thornton, author Judge Max Carlson, Rick Myers, Susan McGrath, Ronnie Rogers, Suzanne Owens and David Guay.

My cousin Shannon Johnson drew the wolf that appears on the book's cover. Her original artwork was sold at auction in Grand Junction, Colorado, to raise funds for her children's elementary school. Shannon gave permission to use her compelling "Howler" for this work.

To my nephew, Eddie Bolger of Boulder, Colorado, and nephew Steve Bolger, and his wife, Libby, of Longmont, Colorado, thank you all for the encouragement. And thanks to the Bolger family, specifically my late parents and late brother and sister-in-law, without whom I would never have visited what we all referred to as the "wolf cabin."

Special tribute also goes to Ruth Glenn, Director of the Colorado State Domestic Violence Program, who has devoted decades to improving and protecting the lives of her fellow domestic-violence victims. Ruth, a graduate of The Women's College at the University of Denver, shared the speaker's podium with me at a co-reunion of her college and Colorado Woman's College, my alma mater. Her personal story of triumph over tragedy inspired many positive traits displayed by characters in *Cry Wolf.*

"The wonder of the wilderness
puts man and his desires into proper perspective."

-Russell H. Varian

1

The Awakening

The small rundown log cabin with its four screen-less windows wide open sits precariously and alone on a high and rocky ridge below a backdrop of rugged mountains. Forty feet lower than the structure rests a beat-up 1980s Ford pickup next to a rusting olive-drab Jeep with a broken windshield. Only tire tracks across the stunted grasses lead into and out of the area. A rocky path provides access by foot to the cabin's splintered and weather-bleached stairs.

A blinding streak of early morning sun slices across the ragged cliffs where aspens and pines sag in the wind and compete for soil at timberline. From one of the cabin's windows, a clear and lyrical woman's voice resonates through the canyon below, "My baby, baby Yupik, Mommy's here! I love you so very, very much."

Contrasting staccato-like echoes bounce back, "...baby, baby, love, very..." as her cooing blends into vague murmurings.

Suddenly, a raspy and angry male voice loudly interjects, "Fer shit's sake, Evie, will ya shut the hell up? Tryin' to sleep! It's five fuckin' thirty in the morning!"

In a more of a whisper and as if she has her face next to that of a child, the woman continues, "Daddy's mad now, sweetie; we have to let Papa Gregg sleep."

After a few seconds, she abruptly screeches, "No, Yupik! Get down! Down! No! No!"

Her words, along with the distinct and unmistakably haunting cry of a wolf, telegraph from the window, piercing the mountain air and instantly setting off howls from what sounds like an entire pack of wolves close by.

Tones ranging from spine-tingling shrieks to baritone moans combine in an eerie cacophony as the once-peaceful dawn erupts with discordant yelping.

Again, the now-enraged voice of the unseen male roars from inside the cabin.

"Evie! Now you've fuckin' done it, damn ya to hell!" his final word loudly echoing, "Hell, hell, hell…"

The form of a what appears to be a thin, middle-aged woman suddenly flees the cabin in a blur and races toward an adjacent enclosed pen. A large adult wolf follows her, trotting at her heels and continuing to cry out. Facing them and turning in circles inside the chain-link enclosure are more than a dozen wolves of various sizes and colors. They nip at one another, bare their fangs, growl briefly, and as the woman calls to them in a guttural language resembling German, they spiral toward her with their tails swishing. Two of the largest, with their heads high, leap over the others, ballet-like, in seeming delight.

In the spreading sunlight, the woman's appearance becomes clear, her face contorting with pain as she lightly rubs her right temple. An area around her eye is dark purple, the eye nearly swollen shut. There are bright red abrasions on her neck and a dark scab covering the tip of her nose. Tears flow down her sun-wrinkled cheeks as she approaches the pen with its ten-foot-high sides.

Despite her pace and a strong upslope breeze, her straw-like dull and matted blond hair clings tightly to her scalp as if a comb might break passing through it.

She wears a faded plaid flannel shirt over worn-thin jeans with ragged cuffs. Her once-expensive leather sandals are ripped and stained, revealing heavily calloused bare feet and long, overgrown and yellowed toenails.

She stumbles forward toward the wolves that have formed a single moving, rippling blanket of gray, light-brown and black. As she approaches them, they appear to recognize her. Two of the smaller ones, whimpering softly in soprano tones, lie down. One pup rolls onto its back in submission. Other wolves lick their lips, bare their teeth in near-smiles and flatten their ears to greet her.

Slowly, the woman chokes out a few more syllables as the wolf that followed her sits sentry-like at her feet.

The wolves, now as a single entity, begin to relax after the Alpha male sounds a final mournful howl and the others immediately go silent, their panting beginning to subside.

Continuing to mumble to the animals in soothing tones, she clinches her rough and grimy fingers through the chain links as the large powerful-looking male slowly ventures forth through his pack, rises up on his back legs to face her, and rests his front paws on the fencing, his amber eyes staring with curiosity directly into the woman's.

Gently he begins to lick her fingertips.

Sobbing, she collapses onto her knees next to Yupik who nuzzles her shaking body.

2

Gasping for Air

On the other side of the mountain range, the top down on her late-model convertible with Texas license plates, an attractive woman in her mid-20s drives steadily through drizzle and low-hanging clouds up the narrow two-lane highway. A young Yellow Labrador sleeps on the passenger's seat beside her.

The moisture on her face highlights her clinched jaw and downturned lips. Both her hands tightly grip the steering wheel and her eyes remain fixed as if in a trance. She doesn't notice the dog's wet fur nor does she appear to see the 18-wheeler carrying a full load of sawn logs barreling toward her from the opposite direction. A blast from its air horn sends her instantly swerving back into her lane, slipping on the wet pavement and almost causing the car to roll. She regains control and wipes sweat from her already dripping forehead.

For the next several miles, still shaking, she passes through rugged and familiar mountains, now consciously focusing on her driving, her ultimate destination and her hoped-for outcome. She looks at the distant mountains and recognizes timberline where the green of the pines abruptly ends and the rocky line of demarcation begins.

When she reads a small highway sign indicating the altitude is 7,000 feet, she states with trepidation to the still-sleeping dog, "We sure aren't in Texas anymore, Destiny!"

In another half hour, she follows a weathered wooden sign onto a sharp turn-off and up a bumpy dirt road to Serenity Lake. Driving higher and higher, she leaves the drizzle and fog below as blue sky fills her vision field. The rising dust combines with the moisture already on everything in her car to form a thin and muddy veneer.

She tries to picture the new life she hopes awaits her, but feels an uncomfortable knot in the pit of her stomach, mentally questioning her decision to leave her successful career in journalism to return alone to her home state. She knows she needs a new start, a clean slate. But as she gets closer to its reality, fear again begins to overtake her.

Breathing becomes more difficult, her heart races, and the surrounding mountains seem to be closing in. As she passes sporadic tire-track dirt lanes with mailboxes positioned alongside the main road, she begins to grind her teeth, discomfort unconsciously setting in when confronting actual civilization. She seems to have forgotten that people still live in these remote mountains, a reality that creates instant distress.

When the car bangs into a large rut in the road, the dog wakes and seems also to sense her anxiety, instantly putting its head onto her lap. She glances down, takes a few shallow breaths, strokes the dog's wet fur and drives on, soon arriving at a well-maintained and modern glass-front cabin about a quarter mile down one of the side roads. She pulls into one of four empty parking spaces separated by large boulders. For several seconds she remains still and takes a few deep breaths before she gets out and begins slowly removing cardboard boxes, small suitcases and household items from the car's trunk. She starts carrying them toward the unoccupied cabin overlooking the lake.

To a casual observer, she might appear to be a fashion model with her flawless skin, red hair beautifully cut, her eyebrows subtly perfect. She wears an expertly fitted white cotton shirt and expensive-looking sculptured jeans that accent her every curve. On a fashion-show runway her body would look right at home, but a closer examination of her face reveals another story.

Sad and dark eyes with half-closed lids gaze emotionlessly, not focusing on anything in particular. Her permanent frown lines announce that this potentially beautiful woman clearly is not at peace.

After making a few trips back and forth from her car, she has also unknowingly spread the thin damp soil that accumulated from her dusty drive, onto her face and blouse, creating an odd contrast of style and shambles.

As she continues to methodically unload the car, stacking its contents on the cabin's porch, she hears a car engine and glances over to see a Cadillac SUV with Montana plates pulling a U-Haul trailer toward the parking area. She feels a pang of jealousy as she sees her brother and sister-in-law inside, realizing they are happy and deeply in love, something she may never experience again. She waves to them, drops the box she's carrying, and jogs over to greet them.

Barely allowing their vehicle to come to a stop, they jump out and run to her. The three join in a long but silent group-hug. She holds tightly to them, her head down. They both kiss her cheeks and wrap their arms tightly around her.

"Laura! Laura!" her sister-in-law declares. "We really wanted to get up here early and have a big welcome ready for you!"

Destiny has raced from person to person begging for attention but getting ignored.

"No worries, Jan," Laura answers. "Just so glad to see you and Ed!"

Both of them notice the grime on her face and blouse but say nothing. Jan takes a tissue from her pocket and gently swipes it over Laura's face, saying, "You've been working hard already, I see! You've already worked up a sweat."

Laura doesn't comment or appear bothered by the attention. Her eyes again indicate she is not in the moment.

After a few seconds, Ed declares, "Actually it was pretty darned good timing! You haven't even opened up the cabin yet."

Handsome, early-30s and athletic, he looks uncomfortably emotional, his eyes glistening, as he quickly turns back to the SUV to open its rear door. He picks up a laptop computer in one arm while easily lifting a large cardboard box in the other. He places the items next to the growing pile on the porch, avoiding eye contact with both women.

Jan, trim and fit, appears close to his same age. She follows him, lugging an especially heavy open box of loose papers that flap in the breeze. She awkwardly bends her head forward to keep the papers in place. Her hair is blond, short and stylish, and she wears a loose-fitting workout outfit with no visible jewelry.

Destiny begins racing from the cars to the porch and back, barking, wagging her tail and getting in the way. Ed, with another load of boxes, jogs onto the porch. Jan follows slowly as Laura struggles with two suitcases and tries to negotiate around Destiny. None of the three seem amused by the dog's antics.

"Destiny, stop it! Now!" Laura loudly scolds.

The dog sits at attention for a few seconds, tilts her head toward Laura and instantly resumes her romp. Laura sighs, shakes her head and says nothing.

"Where do you want your laptop, bedroom or living room?" Ed asks as he opens the front door with one hand, holding the laptop deftly in his other.

"Living room."

"How 'bout these newspaper clippings? The box from hell?" Jan asks hesitantly, looking as if she is trying to read Laura's reaction. "We brought everything here that you shipped to us."

Laura's face suddenly changes as she eyes the box warily. "Next to the fireplace," she says, taking a deliberate and slow breath. "Dr. Marshall, my therapist, says I should go through the stuff, look at it one last time and burn it piece by piece."

"Sis, you sure you don't want us to just take that box back with us to Bozeman? Nothin' says you have to do anything right away," Ed offers, sounding as if he hopes to change her mind.

He starts to wait for her response but instead adds, "Remember, we're just a phone call away and we could bring the box up whenever you're ready."

"Nah. Thanks. I think I'm up to it," Laura, unsmiling, answers as if trying to convince herself. "If not now, when?"

Jan walks through the propped-open door and roughly drops the box onto the hearth as if she's relieved not to be touching it. She hesitates and then picks up a newspaper from the contents' top layer. Its banner headline reads:

**Reporter's Husband Charged in Her
Kidnapping, Attempted Murder**

Jan grimaces, shakes her head as she speed reads the beginning of the story before muttering to herself, "Wanna start the bonfire now? Burn, baby, burn?"

Overhearing her and seeing what Jan holds in her hands, Laura says nothing, just shrugging her shoulders before continuing to focus on unpacking other boxes.

The three continue to work in silence.

Inside the small cabin, it is dark and musty. The drapes are closed. Dusty sheets cover the furniture.

Laura drops the suitcases under a wooden archway connecting a tiny kitchen to a somewhat larger living room. Catching her breath, she sighs again and looks at Ed.

"Lots of memories here, huh? Mostly all good ones, though."

Ed nods, looks around and exhales loudly. He places the laptop on the coffee table and picks up a framed photo from the fireplace mantle. He wipes off the dust with his shirt sleeve to reveal a younger Laura and him, fishing poles in their hands, standing near the lake. Beside them are an older man and woman. Ed sighs and glances sadly at Laura, "Before life beat us up. Last picture of us all together. Can you believe it's been more than a year since anybody's even been up here?"

Laura stares at the floor, says nothing.

He glances briefly over at Jan who winces as if she wishes Ed would change the subject. Taking the photo from Ed's hands, Laura smiles and touches the glass affectionately.

Jan quickly brings the group back to the present, "You sure you don't want us to stay here tonight? Really, I'll call work. We don't want to leave you here alone."

"Thanks. I think I can handle it. Besides, I'm *not* alone. My sweet Destiny's with me. Aren't you girl?"

Hearing her name, Destiny wags her tail and comes to Laura for affection.

"There are much worse things than being alone," Laura states, her eyes glazed over. Then she comes back to reality. "I'm not worried about being alone, but since I just arrived from sea level, I'm starting to feel a little woozy up here. In a day or two, I should adjust to the high altitude."

Destiny again jumps up to Laura, her tail slapping the low table and sending another framed photo Ed has just placed there, crashing to the floor. Laura picks up the frame, containing a photo of herself, happier, younger. The glass has shattered, giving a blurred and distorted perspective.

Ed and Jan look sadly at each other.

"You'll have your hands full with Destiny all right," Jan says.

"Altitude doesn't seem to be affecting her at all!" Ed laughs.

"Lucky dog!" Laura smiles slightly for the first time, as she places the frame back on the coffee table. "But as for staying in touch, I've got email now that the cable was installed, and my cell phone. Place isn't nearly as remote as it once was."

Ed looks uneasy as Laura continues, "And, anyway, nature's always been my best medicine. I'll have everything I need without much of anything."

The three continue to unpack, open drapes and bring light into the rooms. Jan runs a small vacuum over the dusty floors, erasing their footprints.

Through the windows, lush greenery dotted with wild flowers is beginning to bloom just below timberline, now much closer to the cabin's altitude.

After more than two hours, the three stop working, open a small cooler and down soft drinks in silence. No one says a word, but goodbyes are clearly imminent.

The sun has dropped behind the mountains. Long shadows disappear and are replaced by a golden glow. Ed stands, takes one last carton from the now-empty trailer and walks toward Laura who accepts it and places it near the front door.

They exchange hugs. Jan and Ed walk hand-in-hand back toward the SUV followed by Laura and Destiny. As they pass a tree trunk just off the main path, Ed stops and points, "Hey, look at that. It's the tree we thought was dead and Dad sawed it down to the trunk. Now look at those green sprouts coming out of its side!"

Laura stops to look.

"I can't believe this!" Laura says, smiling at Ed. "I always loved that pine tree. Remember when you and I used to decorate it every Christmas? Then it turned brown and we were sure it was dead. Now look what's happening!"

"Nature's amazing!" Jan adds as they arrive at the SUV. Ed climbs into the driver's seat. Jan waves and pulls herself up into the passenger side.

Laura, with Destiny at her feet, watches them drive away as a hint of dust rises from the car as it disappears into the distance.

As Laura walks back toward the cabin, the dim light from the kitchen provides the only indication of civilization anywhere around the lake. Just overhead, she spots the alternating red and green lights on the wingtips on a low-flying small plane, its engine purring a reassuring sound. The plane's pilot and any passengers onboard would have a clear view of the lakeshore ringed in tall pine trees interspersed with the light gray bark of leafless aspen trees reaching up toward them.

In the afterglow, with a light blanket draped around her shoulders, Laura sits quietly on a well-worn wooden chair on the porch, petting Destiny.

"A new life in an old familiar place," she thinks to herself.

3

Not Undercover

His room, an end unit in the Big Timber Motel, looks larger than most. Although not spacious, it includes a kitchen, a full bath with tub and stall shower, and a living room with two large chairs and a convertible sofa facing an outdated console television set.

A separate bedroom, more crowded with its king-sized bed and large closet, has a new flat-screen television on the wall facing the bed. Off the kitchen is a back door leading to a small patio where two chairs await occupants desiring a view of the distant mountains, the plastic surfaces badly streaked where accumulated dust has met afternoon rains.

The atmosphere inside is stark, almost like a military barracks. No personal items are visible, not a photo, a set of keys, a dirty coffee cup or a scuffed pair of shoes. Only one small area provides a hint as to who its resident is. On the top of the nightstand rests a loaded .45 caliber automatic in a well-oiled leather holster alongside a polished gold badge from the county sheriff's department. Next to the badge is a metal nametag: Captain Duane Armstrong.

The small digital clock on the table shows 1:30 a.m. and the shower can be heard running in the bathroom. When he emerges with a large white towel wrapped around his waist, Duane begins his routine. He clicks on the living room television, turns down its volume to nearly inaudible and walks back to the bathroom to dry his hair, leaning out to watch the old set. Next, he returns to the bedroom, pulls open a dresser drawer, takes out a pair of neatly folded pajamas, puts them on while turning off the console and turning on the flat screen set.

Continuing the routine, he removes the bedspread, carefully folds it and places it on a chair. The bed itself looks as if it is awaiting military inspection when the officer in charge drops a quarter onto the tightly tucked-in sheets and blanket to see if it will bounce. Using the remote he turns up the volume. He pulls out a heating pad from under the bed, places two pillows against the headboard, climbs onto the bed and leans against the pad, which is positioned precisely in the small of his back.

He sleeps off and on glancing at the television until 6 a.m. when, without an alarm sounding, he energetically gets out of bed, smoothes the sheets, fluffs the pillows and replaces the bedspread perfectly. He tosses his pajamas into a laundry bag, quickly showers again, shaves and puts on his perfectly ironed uniform. In less than 20 minutes, he climbs into the sheriff's department's four-door patrol car parked outside and drives the mile to Crystal's Cafe where the cardboard CLOSED sign on the front door has just been removed and the red and blue neon OPEN sign in the window has begun to flash.

It is exactly 6:30 as he comes through the door.

Crystal, the 60-something owner, has his coffee cup already filled, his cooked breakfast of two scrambled eggs and one strip of bacon with wheat toast sitting on a plate next to a folded newspaper in the first booth. He is unsmiling as he waves routinely to Crystal and picks up the newspaper, immediately starting to read.

To anyone observing him, he's just a regular cop—40s, tall, ruggedly handsome, well-built and with a touch of gray in his well-cut hair. He is totally focused on the task at hand, a real professional.

A more observant person might also notice his eyes look sad and his demeanor seems slightly angry.

An attractive, well-dressed woman in her 30s enters the empty cafe minutes after Duane begins reading his newspaper. She chooses the booth facing his and smiles, speaking in a friendly tone as he glances up and they have instant eye contact, "Morning, officer!"

Crystal, approaching the woman with a glass of water and a menu, hears her greeting and looks at Duane, expecting his response.

He says nothing, looks back down and continues to read, holding his coffee cup up to signal Crystal for a refill.

She quickly interjects, "Good morning!" to the woman, and smiles as she hands her a menu and places the water glass on the table.

Returning to Duane's booth, Crystal tops off his coffee, shakes her head and whispers to him,"Well, we can sure as hell see that Officer Armstrong is one happy camper this morning!"

Duane pushes his newspaper aside, drops a handful of singles on the table, stands, grabs his hat and quickly walks out the door.

Once in the patrol car, he hits the steering wheel with both hands, scowls and spits out, "Damned women! Can't even eat in peace!"

He starts the engine.

4

Flashing Back

The sun is rising. Laura wears a new pair of running shoes, gray sports pants, a light jacket and a small backpack. She carries a rustic hand-carved wooden walking stick and proceeds at a brisk pace. Checking her watch, she sees it's 6:30. Following Dr. Marshall's advice to force positive thoughts into her mind each day, especially at the time she's exercising, she directs her mind to the night she received the first-place award for newspaper feature writing from the Texas Bureau of the Associated Press for her series of articles on modern-day mid-wives.

As she relives hearing her name called by the master of ceremonies, she instantly feels the same excitement she experienced that night.

Dr. Marshall told her to remember, "Your mind only goes where you tell it to. Happiness is a choice!"

Suddenly, she realizes she has been missing that unique sense of fulfillment. Nothing in her life has been good since then, not her family, her marriage, her interactions.

Destiny trots alongside her as they travel down the dirt road with no visible traffic in either direction. A half mile behind them is her family cabin.

The dog begins to dart from the road to the adjacent ditch, then venture to the edges of the cattle pasture, excitedly sniffing and exploring.

Blue sky, mountain views and clear air abound. Laura stops to take in the atmosphere and then resumes her walk. Her strides are long, her head high. Just when she starts to feel somewhat normal, she hears a vehicle approaching behind her. She steps to the side of the road, calling to Destiny.

"Come here, girl!" she says firmly as the dog slows, looks back at her and continues exploring. Concerned, Laura demands loudly, "Now, Destiny! Right now!"

The dog trots back.

A dusty, late-model pickup truck with an empty gun rack visible in its cab, slows down as it approaches her. The driver, a 20-something guy wearing a cowboy hat, checks out Laura. He beeps the horn, smiles and waves.

Her mood and demeanor immediately change. She drops the walking stick and turns and abruptly heads directly towards the cows grazing in the pasture parallel to the road. Her heart beats wildly. She gasps for breath. She begins to shiver suddenly and rubs her arms. She stops and stares into the distance, her back to the pickup as if that will make it disappear.

The pickup speeds up and continues down the road, dust rising into the early morning air. Laura starts to hear voices that take her back to Texas. It isn't the first time:

A policeman in uniform is on the stand giving testimony in a courtroom. Laura sits in the front row, slumped over slightly, head in her hands, listening. The policeman says, "We got a 911 call at the station from a guest in the Lone Star Inn saying that he heard a commotion in the next room and said he saw a man acting suspiciously. He said the man was carrying something to his truck, either a body or a rolled-up carpet. Something heavy, he said, wrapped up."

Laura, feeling dizzy, grasps the split-rail fence as her mind suddenly returns to the courtroom:

The prosecuting attorney, a tall woman in a dark business suit with a clipboard in her hand, interrupts the testimony to ask, "The Lone Star Inn? Would you tell the court what kind of a hotel or motel that is and if you had ever been called out there previously?

The officer raises his eyebrows and says, "We get calls from there routinely, almost every night or sometimes twice a night. It's rundown and cheap and attracts homeless people, drug addicts, prostitutes. Every officer on the force has been called there on police matters."

The prosecutor asks, "Was the call on July 14th of last year taken seriously?"

Checking a written report he is holding, the officer uses his finger to trace down a list, "Of course, we take all 911 calls seriously but we have priorities and the Lone Star wasn't at the top of the list that night.

He pauses to find his place on the sheet and continues, "We had two vehicle accidents with injuries, a domestic violence call and a hold-up at a convenience store all around the same time. We didn't make it to the Lone Star until after 4 a.m., about 20 minutes after the caller had checked out.

"Besides, drunks and addicts often report seeing lots of strange things. We show up and they have forgotten they even called us."

"Did you ask the front desk for the caller's name or whereabouts?"

"Yes, and they said he was there just a couple hours, a John Doe, paid in advance and left the key in the room without stopping by the office."

"Please continue. Describe how and when you located the victim and how the connection to the Lone Star Inn was ultimately made."

"We got another call about 8 a.m. from the office of the Restful Oaks Cemetery who said an Hispanic man, a grave digger who was preparing a grave for an afternoon funeral, heard something coming from inside a small mausoleum building right next to where he was working."

With the pickup's engine becoming more faint as it disappears in the dust around a curve in the road, Laura resumes walking as if stunned, her legs weak and shaking. She briefly closes her eyes tightly, opens them again and shakes her head back to the present, then turns around and walks back to the road, forgetting to pick up her hiking stick.

Startled, she looks down and realizes the cold moist thing touching her hand is Destiny's nose. The dog whimpers, her head cocked as if puzzled. Laura reaches into her jacket pocket, takes out a treat and tosses it to Destiny.

The two walk on together.

5

Day Is Done

Inside the cabin, Laura sits at the kitchen table. Suddenly, she feels the chills coming on again but knows it is not the flu or any physical illness. She tries to take her mind to a happier time and place but it doesn't work. She knows the symptoms; it's happening again. She rubs her arms and blots her sweaty forehead with a paper napkin and then resumes eating a now-room-temperature frozen dinner, its box and plastic wrap laying on the table next to her.

The microwave oven door is open, its light the only illumination in the room. She decides to force her mind away from the nightmarish past and concentrate on the simple, positive present. She inhales and she speaks to Destiny fast asleep under the table at her feet. She slowly reaches down to pet her head.

"Pretty good start, huh, girl? Wore you out, didn't I?"

Destiny snores away and Laura smiles.

While continuing to eat with her slightly shaking right hand, she pulls a cell phone from her jeans with her left and punches in a number. A few seconds pass as she nervously drums her fingers on the phone.

"Hi, Ed. It's me. What ya up to?"

"Laura! Just watching television. How ya doing, kiddo? Adjusting to the altitude?"

Consciously trying to sound upbeat, she answers, "I'm fine. In fact, Destiny and I hiked from the cabin all the way to Box Canyon and back today. Felt good."

"Great!" Ed responds with enthusiasm. "The exercise will do you good! See anybody on the road?"

Suddenly, Laura closes her eyes, visualizes the pickup, bites her lower lip and clinches her fists. She opens her eyes and mouth at once without answering the question and blurts out, "I want to put my computer together tonight. Did you see the connector cables?"

"Try the box from hell," Ed says, not mentioning he has noticed her avoiding his question. "I'm pretty sure the cables are at the bottom."

Hesitantly she peers over at the box on the fireplace hearth. Her left foot and lower leg begins to twitch uncontrollably, knocking into Destiny, who wakes up, looks up at her and moves away.

"Okay, thanks," she says, trying to sound neutral, if not positive. "I'll email ya."

"Bye, Sis, take care."

Clicking off the phone, she stands and inches toward the box, reaches out, stops, turns and immediately heads in the opposite direction. She walks to the bedroom where the bed remains covered with a dusty sheet. Folded blankets, clean sheets and pillows sit on a chair ready to be put to use. She picks them up and then suddenly throws the entire stack onto the floor.

She returns to the couch where a pillow and light wool throw are bunched to one side, looking used from the night before. She closes the microwave door and plops down in the pitch black fully clothed.

Destiny ambles over and settles down on the floor next to the couch.

6

Horse Sense

The sun is up and starting to warm the 40-degree air as Destiny and Laura walk along a dirt road next to a ranch. Horses nibble grass in a pasture parallel to the road. Numerous Black Angus cows with young calves graze in several fenced-in areas nearby. In the distance, a large two-story ranch house loosely circled by a dozen or more one-story log cabins, comes into view. The cabins, dotting the acreage each sport well-bleached deer antlers nailed above their front doors.

After another quarter mile, Laura stops and smiles up at an obviously hand-made but attractive knotty pine sign with large contrasting black wooden letters spelling out, *TIMBERLINE RANCH*, arching over the entry road. Out-of-state cars crowd the parking area. Laura hangs onto the split-rail fence and gazes at the horses in the adjacent pasture. She feels at peace, calm, just as she had hoped she would. She begins consciously to inhale the mountain air, watching as the horses flip their tails and graze on the tender green grasses. As contentment starts to sweep over her, she relaxes her shoulders. Her eyes close.

Suddenly Destiny destroys the mood as she crawls under a broken part of the fence, races toward the horses, and begins loud, non-stop barking. The horses scatter. One black gelding simultaneously kicks both back legs dangerously close to Destiny's head as she chases after him.

Laura shouts, "Damn it, Destiny! Come back here! Now!"

A tanned, chiseled-face cowboy in his late 40s with a bridle in one hand, tries to catch one of the horses Destiny has just spooked, but the horse is heading for the other side of the pasture. The cowboy does not look happy.

Not seeing Laura, he runs toward Destiny to scare her, kicking dirt at her with a well-worn boot. "Get the hell outta here! Ya hear me? Get! Ya damned mutt!"

Laura calls to the cowboy and waves, sounding apologetic, "I'm really sorry. Come here, Destiny!"

Destiny races back to her.

The cowboy ignores both the dog and Laura and concentrates on trying to coax another of the horses over to him. He stretches out his hand, holding a sugar cube in it. A black and white Pinto seems interested and begins to stroll his way.

The bridle is soon on and the cowboy leads the horse to an adjoining corral. He continues to ignore everything else around and seems disinterested in socializing.

Laura who has climbed over the fence and Destiny, now calm, both walk toward him.

She attempts to explain, "I apologize. She's a city pooch. Hasn't seen horses before. Hope we didn't mess you up."

He doesn't respond to her comment or look at her or at the dog. He begins to saddle the horse, hauling a scuffed western saddle and faded saddle blanket off the fence and slinging them onto the Pinto's back. As he begins to tighten the cinch, he glances up at Laura and immediately notices her good looks. His demeanor changes. He's clearly rattled and begins to talk fast, "Where ya'll from? Ya stayin' here at the ranch? Hadn't seen ya before."

"Well, I came up here from Texas, most recently. And no my dog and I aren't staying here. But my family's had a cabin on Lake Serenity for years. Spent lots of time at the Timberline's square dances when I was much younger."

He smiles, nods his head in amusement, "We still have them ever' Saturday night. Live western band and all. Dudes love 'em."

She nods, remembering.

"I'm a Madonna holdout, myself," he adds, looking to see if her face changes at his comment.

Laura's face is blank. He notices she looks unhappy, uncomfortable, as if she has something to say but is waiting for the right time.

He continues to prepare the horses as she watches in silence. Several saddled swayed-backs soon stand tied to the corral's fence.

"By the way, I'm Laura," she says finally, trying to keep eye contact with him and extending her hand and not taking it back when he does not immediately reach to shake it.

Her years of being a newspaper reporter have taught her how to get information from people who are reluctant to divulge it or even talk to her. She realizes she may need to butter him up a bit. Persistence pays off, she has learned.

"Jerry," he says, removing his dirty leather glove and then wiping his hand on his jeans before shaking hers.

"Question for ya," she says, almost sounding like a cowgirl herself.

He starts to lead another horse toward those tied to the corral railing. He stops.

"Shoot," he says, gazing again at her with continued appreciation.

"Think I could arrange to rent a horse just to ride myself? Or do I have to go on an official trail ride with the dudes?" she says, forcing a smile.

Jerry looks disappointed that the social interaction has so quickly turned to business. His tone becomes more official. "Sorry. Don't really rent to the public. Need our horses for the dudes, er, sorry, ranch guests we're supposed to call 'em."

"Oh, well, I tried," Laura says as her smile evaporates. She looks at the ground.

He sees her disappointment.

When she sighs deeply and walks over to pet the Pinto, Jerry notices she is more than comfortable with the horse, as she wraps her arm around its neck and pats it gently.

"Done much ridin'?"

"Since I was six when I got a pony for Christmas. After that all through school I had horses and did some amateur rodeos. Never won a thing, though." She stares off into the distance as if reliving another frustrating part of her past.

But Jerry seems impressed at what he has heard. He takes off his hat and scratches his head. He looks as if he wants to help solve her problem.

"How long ya want to rent one for?"

She answers immediately, "By the day, week, or month. Whatever works. Plan to be up here from now all through the summer. Maybe permanently. I'd be happy to saddle it myself, curry it, whatever you say."

He continues to stare at Laura without speaking.

"I'd also return it to the barn or pasture, wherever you want," she adds, hoping to convince him of her willingness.

He begins to weaken. "Tell ya what. I'll ask the boss. Come on by tomorrow and look for me. Vince Williams is my manager. I'll ask him tonight. He's busy now. Can't promise ya anything, though."

He sticks out his hand to shake hers again and asks,

"What did you say your last name was?"

Laura, seeming startled by his question, stutters when she tries to say her last name.

"Um, I'm Laura Black, er, Laura Bell."

She quickly points at the dog, "This is Destiny. You've already met her. Unfortunately, she was not on her best behavior."

Jerry notices her nervousness and discomfort but says nothing.

Destiny tries to coax Jerry into petting her, sitting at his feet and wagging her tail. He finally gives in.

7

Boxed In

A few hours later, Laura sits on the couch staring again at the cardboard box on the hearth. Her hands sweat. Her eyes start to flood with tears. She is back in court hearing the policeman's voice. Again.

"It was an old mausoleum building that wasn't just for urns of ashes but also could accommodate a full-sized coffin. Since it actually ends up costing more than a regular burial plot, and the cemetery is also pretty rundown, there are lots of open, unused compartments.

The officer continues, "The grave digger was really freaking out on the phone and we were told by the dispatcher to respond right away. When we got there, he had already removed the door on one particular unit of the mausoleum. Inside we could see a large metal tool box." He refers again to a sheet of paper. "The tool box measured five feet nine by 20 inches deep and 18 inches high, one of those that go all the way across the bed of a standard pickup truck."

Some of the jury members lean forward in their seats. Every eye is on the officer. Ed and Jan sit on either other side of Laura. Ed holds her hand; Jan has her arm around Laura's shoulder, pulling her close.

After a deep breath, Laura stands slowly, then painfully inches over toward the fireplace and kneels down, cautiously touching the cardboard box beside the hearth as if it might burn her. She begins taking out the folded newspaper on top. As she reads, she again is transported back in time. She stares through the newspaper not at it, her eyes focusing beyond the printed page.

A large front-page color photo shows Laura unable to walk and almost being lifted up completely by two police officers, her arms across each of their shoulders, her legs dragging limply through the weedy cemetery. A piece of duct tape that had been across her mouth dangles from one side of her cheek. It appears to have been pulled back to help her breathe during her rescue.

Next to it is a second photo, taken in front of a jail, showing Al Black, identified as Laura's husband, handcuffed and walking between two police officers, each firmly gripping his arms.

Her mind has gone blank. She doesn't move for a few seconds. When she comes back to the present, she realizes she has just crushed the newspaper, nearly tearing it in half. She places it face down on the hearth.

She reaches back inside the box and lifts out a large white photo album, unwraps the plastic cover and slowly opens the album. She glances at the first page and quickly clutches it to her breast and holds it as if she will never release it.

After several minutes, she pulls it away to stare closely at the photo. It is of her in a wedding dress standing at the altar with Al. She looks radiant and Al is smiling. She bites her lip, grimaces, then slams the album shut and angrily pushes the box away.

Destiny, hearing the commotion, trots into the room, leans up next to her and licks her hand.

Laura slowly picks up the newspaper again, stuffs it into the fireplace, opens the flue and lights the paper. Large flames reflect in her eyes. Sighing heavily, she sits down in front of the fire and feels herself begin to relax.

Destiny lies down and puts her head on Laura's leg.

"We really needed this fire!" Laura says to Destiny with a shadow of a smile. She gets down onto her knees and pushes the wedding-photo album under the couch and out of sight.

Through the window, she can see a spring storm has started to darken the sky. Light rain begins to fall.

After a few minutes, Laura digs back down into the box and removes several computer cables.

8

Tears Are Only Rain

Laura types on her laptop with a small printer attached to it in the living room, leaning over the coffee table in an awkward position. For the first time in a long time, she looks more positive, more in control, back in her element: writing. Heavy rain begins to batter the roof as her fingers race over the keyboard and words begin to fly. The power of the storm seems exhilarating. Destiny looks up with curiosity. In 11111111111111111111seconds the screen is filled:

Greetings, Josie.

Want you to know I'm in big sky country. Free at last! I can finally breathe. One thing I hadn't counted on feeling, though. This is the first time I haven't had a job since I was 16. Feels weird. What will I do with my days, my nights? Money doesn't help what ails me. Hope all's well with you way over there in D.C.

Cheers! Your Roomie

Without re-reading the paragraph, she pushes SEND, waits a few seconds, then turns off the computer. She looks relieved. Out on the porch, she stands stretching her arms over her head. The rain has stopped. The air is clean, fresh, new. Stars appear. She plops down on a soaking wet wooden chair with Destiny lying at her feet, when suddenly she notices the dog's ears perk up; Destiny has become acutely alert.

"What is it, girl?" Laura says, sitting forward on the damp chair.

Then from some distance away, she hears distinct howling. It is a chorus, not one of the victory howls she has heard over the years after a pack of coyotes makes a kill, but a mournfully discomforting choir of high and low yowlings which continues to disturb, to unsettle.

Laura shudders, listens. The howling fades into yelping. She stands to return inside and calls to Destiny who sits up frozen in place, her eyes fixed. Head cocked, Destiny begins to whine loudly as if trying to figure out how to answer the howls. She rises to all fours and starts to walk slowly in the direction of the cries.

Laura grabs her collar just in time and pulls her back toward the door, saying in a reassuring tone, "Just coyotes, girl. Come on, let's go in."

But, Laura, too, is drawn to the compelling sounds and stops to look back.

9

Decision Day

Outside Timberline Ranch, there is a flurry of activity. Cars, pick-ups and SUVs crowd the parking lot. Laura, in a denim skirt, white blouse and a tightly pulled-down western hat, the brim of which rests on her designer sunglasses, drives in with the convertible's top down. Destiny rides shotgun. They both look as if they have a mission to accomplish.

Laura has purposely dressed in western garb and has applied more makeup than usual, trying to influence Jerry and perhaps Vince if she gets to meet him. She needs to make a good impression. Renting a horse is a big part of the recovery plan she has constructed with Dr. Marshall's help, and Timberline Ranch, the only dude ranch within a half day's drive, is her only prospect. She slows down and parks.

Destiny doesn't wait until Laura opens the door and instead leaps out from her place on the front seat and trots directly toward the corral where Jerry is saddling an Appaloosa. Two ranch guests in new cowboy hats, western shirts and starched un-faded jeans watch him with interest.

Laura shouts, "Destiny! No! Sit!"

The dog stops in her tracks.

Somewhat startled to simultaneously see the dog and hear Laura's command, Jerry looks up, sees she's dressed fit to kill and he blurts out, "Say, not bad. I'm damned impressed!"

Then he catches himself gawking only at Laura as she exits the car and begins looking at the dog, adding, "Destiny, is, er, learnin'!"

He smiles as Laura approaches. She walks over to Destiny and gives her a treat and pats her head.

The clink of horseshoes rises from the guest recreational area along with some shrill voices of those involved in the competition.

Small children splash gleefully in a wading pool ringed by chatting mothers on lounge chairs. Laura stares at the children and their mothers and a pang of sadness sweeps over her. Will she ever be any child's mother? She quickly looks away as an older man and woman slowly ride by on horses. Will she ever be anyone's partner?

Jerry finishes the saddling and walks over to greet her. "Good news!" he says, smiling. "Boss says if you want to rent by the month, he'll give you a good price—only two fifty. Okay? But, you gotta sign an agreement, ya know. Them lawyers never quit!" he shakes his head, taking out a ballpoint pen and a folded and slightly wrinkled paper from his shirt pocket.

Laura looks delighted and reaches to take the paper and pen. She realizes she's the happiest she's been since she arrived at the cabin and the most animated in more than a year.

"Deal!" she agrees, quickly scribbling her signature onto the paper. She takes out a blank check from her skirt pocket and writes in the amount and hands Jerry the paper, the check, and the pen.

Looking pleased, Jerry boasts, "Vince's even gonna give you his own horse, too. Solo's his name. A Palomino. Nice trail horse. Vince don't never let dudes ride 'im, but I told him you had experience."

"Great! Thanks, Jerry. I really appreciate your help. So, when can I meet Solo?

"How's 'bout now?"

Laura looks down at her new leather heels and quickly pulls out a pair of bright yellow "Crocs" from a large bag she's carrying. She planned for this contingency.

Jerry stares at her shapely legs as she lifts her skirt and balances on one foot, then the other, slipping out of good shoes and into the washable ones. She tosses the heels into the bag as the two walk side-by-side toward the barn.

Laura has a noticeable bounce in her step.

"So why'd you say you left Texas to come up here?" Jerry asks with new familiarity.

Staring straight ahead, Laura, close-to-the-vest, answers immediately, "I didn't say."

Jerry shrugs, avoids eye contact, and continues forward to the barn.

10

Clean Sweep

Josephine, an attractive mid-20s Italian-American, sits at her computer keyboarding an email. The U.S. Capitol can be seen through her office window. A color photo on her desk shows her with Laura, wearing green and white sweatshirts and standing in front of the college's historic Treat Hall in Denver with its 1888 red-brick cornerstone between them.

Laura:

You sound great on email but I'll need the latest iPhone or Skype to see for sure. Gotta hear your voice, look you in the face, in the eyes. Seriously, though, I'm so proud of you for doing it alone. Don't know if I could. You're my hero! BTW, remember our old-fart psych prof who told us the actual condition of the inside of your car reflects your life and your state of mind? Well, guess what? My car's filthy dirty! lol Gotta run.

Love, Jo

Laura reads Jo's email, smiles slightly as she looks outside her window and in the moonlight sees her own car with its convertible top securely up and its doors locked, knowing it is perfectly safe, freshly cleaned, and organized.

"I sure hope our old prof was right!" she thinks to herself.

She turns off the laptop and picks up a magazine to read and then puts it down. She then opens a book but never looks at it. Then she takes the remote and clicks it. She begins to stare at the screen without blinking. Her breathing becomes rapid. She suddenly starts to shake uncontrollably as she again hears the prosecutor's question to the policeman in court.

"Officer, what did you find when you and your partner arrived at Restful Oaks Cemetery?"

"We got there in less than five minutes and when we drove up, the man was frantic. The crypt was about eye level with him and the metal box was too heavy for him to lift out by himself. He was trying to break the big lock on the tool box with his shovel. We got out of the patrol car and ran to him."

"What did he say to you?" the prosecutor asks.

"At first, he was so freaked out we could barely understand him, but he was gasping and pointing inside the metal box. Then we realized what he was yelling to us was, 'Alive! Person alive!' "

Laura jumps up from the couch, grabs her cell phone and punches automatic dial. She begins to pace back and forth.

After a few seconds she hears someone answer and blurts out, "Dr. Marshall? It's Laura Black, um, I mean, Laura Bell. I know it's late, but."

In his house, Ron Marshall, 50s, still prone, reaches over and picks up the phone. He rubs his eyes, looks at the digital clock which displays 1:40 a.m. and speaks with a groggy voice.

"It's okay. It's okay. Calm down. Calm down. Sorry, um, who is this?"

"Laura. Laura Black."

He sits straight up in bed. His wife first looks alarmed, then turns on the nightstand light.

"You said to call if I ever needed to. Having a panic attack," she says, her voice sounding girlish and shy. She also sounds completely out of breath.

Marshall's wife rolls over face down and covers her head with her pillow. Seems as though she's been here, done this before.

He rubs his eyes again and fumbles for his glasses, while sounding reassuring, "Calm down, Laura! Take a couple deep breaths, then talk to me."

"Um. Okay, okay," she closes her eyes, takes deliberate and loud deep breaths, exhales. "Okay. Okay. I'm, I'm, uh, okay."

Dr. Marshall, now sitting with his feet on the floor, is holding his bald head with one hand, the phone with the other, and is attempting to open his eyes.

Laura starts to speak but is still somewhat out of breath and frantic, "No flashbacks for a while. Thought I was getting over this. It's been almost six months."

She pauses again. After a few seconds, she seems calmer.

"But I've had three attacks in three days! Another one tonight! I took your advice. I'm safe and in a place with lots of good memories. Purging the bad ones, like you said. Piece by piece."

Marshall interrupts, "And did you do any writing about Al, or writing him directly and telling him he's no longer part of your life, your world? Then burning what you wrote?"

She says nothing.

"Laura? You know we practiced that and it was helping you. Also try to practice using your maiden name. Bell!"

His tone is firm.

Sounding like a little girl whose teacher has just asked why she hasn't done her homework, Laura answers in a voice higher than usual, "Um. I know. I need to do that. Just need to break the habit."

"Work on that Laura!" he says sternly. "It will make you return to being your own self and extricate your life from Al Black's.

"And what else did I also tell you to always do?" Marshall asks in a slow, patronizing tone.

His wife groans, grabs her pillow and staggers from their bedroom. She can see it may be a long night.

Laura begins to feel calmer. She sits down. Destiny comes to her and puts her head in Laura's lap.

"I know. I know. Always do what I'm afraid to do at least once a day. That's why I'm up here. Thanks, doctor. Sorry. I'm okay now, I think. Just needed to hear you say it, hear your voice."

"Who's there with you, Laura? Your brother? You're not alone are you? Are you up in Montana like you planned?"

"Yes," she answers softly, looking guiltily at Destiny as if the dog could recognize the "sin of omission" of her not revealing the whole truth to Dr. Marshall.

"Good. Don't try to face all this alone. That's not what I mean by doing something that scares you. Take baby steps. And remember what I said about the cry-wolf syndrome. Watch that very carefully and get all the facts, remember?"

"Thanks, Doctor Marshall. I'll try. I'm better now. Sorry to wake you up! Good night."

"Night, Laura. Take care. Remember, you can do this."

She clicks off the cell phone and takes a few more deep breaths. She walks over to the box near the fireplace and removes some greeting cards tied with ribbon. She reads each one slowly, then tosses it into the fireplace where a small fire burns. She crumples a large pink card with a red satin valentine heart on its front. She watches big flames go up. As they turn to ash, she angrily throws in most of the rest of that bundle, keeping a special few secured in a silver ribbon. She looks sad, then relieved.

Collecting together the remaining cards, she pushes them under the couch.

The only light in the room comes from the glowing embers in the fire. She watches them for a while and then curls up with her blanket and pillow on the couch in the living room. As she does, she remembers feeling the safety of Dr. Marshall's office couch when he talked in soothing tones to her and gave her what he obviously felt were final pieces of advice just before she left for Montana.

He instructed her in ways to consciously avoid a syndrome he believed many victims betrayed by loved ones or victims of domestic violence often experience. He called it cry-wolf behavior.

Trying to recall the characteristics he described, one thing comes into her mind. He had warned her that some domestic-violence victims who have the syndrome are often convinced they are always 100% right about judging people or events when every scrap of evidence points to a totally different conclusion or direction, sometimes 180 degrees.

"Don't bore me with the facts; my mind's made up," Marshall quoted, telling her it was an old saying but something she needed to watch when starting to trust people again.

She thought at the time it was unnecessary advice and couldn't grasp why he felt he needed to repeat it on the phone.

Feeling sleepy now and hearing those words in her mind made her even more positive that she, a former professional journalist, who spent years learning how to be objective by gathering facts and being trained to present two sides to every story, would never succumb to that subjective and flawed way of thinking. Surely, he was talking about something that couldn't happen to her. It seemed insulting.

11

Morning Has Broken

It's misting lightly. Fog hovers over the lake. Destiny and Laura eat breakfast. Both have bowls of dry food in front of them. Looking down at her next to the table, Laura notices and offers, "Want some on yours, too?" as she pours the milk onto her own Chocolate Cheerios.

Destiny keeps crunching away at her kibbles and remains totally focused on her bowl.

Soon, they're both in the car heading up the dirt road toward Timberline Ranch. She drives with the top down and Destiny in her usual position. They're both damp from the drive, as are the upholstery and dashboard. She parks and strolls toward the corral. Destiny runs ahead.

Jerry unloads hay bales from a ranch pickup as Madonna's music blares from the truck's cab. When he sees Laura, he tips his Stetson.

Laura looks great in tight jeans, a western shirt, her cowboy hat, boots. Jerry notices. She waves at him.

"How come ya always drive with the top down? Gonna ruin them fancy car seats. Gonna rain big-time today fer sure."

Laura seems annoyed at his comments and says nothing. Momentarily she feels herself confined and restricted in the tool box. She knows she will die there alone.

Jerry sees the pained expression on her face and is puzzled.

Her demeanor doesn't invite further questions but in a few seconds, she reacts, locks eyes with him and sounds normal.

"Any chance I can take Solo out today?" she asks enthusiastically.

He gestures toward the largest stall in the barn, "You know where he's at. Go for it!"

Jerry walks toward the barn, stops and gestures up toward the base of the mountain. "Just one thing, though. Vince wants you to stay on the ranch property at all times. Somethin' about our insurance."

Looking somewhat surprised, Laura agrees, "Fine. Whatever he says."

"Gotta another rule around here. Don't go above timberline either. Period. Plenty of great trails around here without goin' too far up. And, of course, dismount your horse in thunderstorms."

She nods.

He points upward to ominous gathering clouds.

She again looks puzzled but just nods. She looks up at the nearest mountain with its distinct timberline. To her, it looks as if it would take days of riding for someone on horseback to get there.

"No worries," she adds.

As Jerry starts to walk away, he turns and adds, "Used to be lots of hippies up in there. Most of them is gone, but just in case, Vince don't want our dudes to have nothin' to do with 'em. They're probably all too stoned to cause anybody trouble, but just in case, he told me to tell you to always stay on the ranch."

As she scans the foothills, a few rain clouds hover. She returns to her car and pushes the button to close the convertible top. Once it's secured, she walks back to the barn. The mountains have begun to change again from friendly looking to threatening. A hint of thunder rumbles in the distance.

"Guess we'll steer clear today," she calls to Jerry. "Probably won't ride Solo after all. Looks like a thunderstorm brewing."

Jerry nods and goes about his chores.

Laura heads for her car looking back somewhat longingly at a horse trail. Destiny trots beside her. As she drives out of the ranch parking lot, huge rain drops begin to fall. She puts the top back down. Destiny sits on the passenger seat, leaning outward, her head in the breeze, blinking back the rain. They pass an old hay wagon sporting a hand-lettered cardboard sign with its Magic Marker message starting to blur and drip, *"Hay Ride Tonight at 6 with BBQ."*

Laura mutters to Destiny as if the dog can read, "Not for us. We'll have to take a rain check, won't we?"

12

Trail Trials

Laura, dressed in a baseball cap, sweatshirt, jeans and sturdy cowboy boots, mounts Solo.

Jerry stands next to the horse gesturing toward the foothills again as he gives her more instructions.

The sun is up and only a few dark clouds remain from the previous night's rain. She looks serious as she listens. Even Destiny, sitting completely still at Jerry's feet, seems to be at attention.

"Like I was tellin' ya, that far trail's the one we use for the dudes. Nice and gentle loop. It'll give ya time to get acquainted with Solo. He's used to Vince. Nobody else ever rides 'im."

She pats Solo's neck as he moves nervously under her. He pulls on the bit and the reins slip through Laura's hands, stinging them, reminding her she forgot her riding gloves.

"Might even see some big-horn sheep if you're lucky. Takes about three hours, start to finish. Passes an old grave yard."

Laura, taking mental notes, nods, consciously choosing to ignore his comment about the cemetery.

"Got your rain gear along just in case?"

She points behind her saddle where a red-hooded wind breaker is rolled up and tied on with the saddle straps. She waves goodbye and urges Solo to walk while speaking softly, "Okay, Solo boy, let's go exploring."

Destiny remains sitting next to Jerry, looking uncertain as to how to proceed. Laura calls to her and she eagerly follows Solo out of the corral and onto a muddy trail full of deep ruts and horse droppings.

As she peers ahead over the horse's ears at the trail, Laura remembers reading a comment about horses and how they have affected man's history. Over time, from princes to paupers, everyone, in one way or another, has depended on the horse for farming, travel, transporting crops, wars, recreation, even gambling. And now, Laura is keenly aware that she, too, is depending on a horse. This time for healing.

Above timberline, a big-horn sheep's view down at the loop trail would show Laura on Solo with Destiny trotting alongside and slowly proceeding higher and higher into the mountains.

After two hours, they begin to straddle timberline. The sun peeks through the clouds. Light rain becomes intermittent. She is soon wearing her wind breaker with its hood covering her hair. The phrase, "Little red riding hood," comes into her head and repeats as if on a continuous audio loop.

Destiny appears happy, if soggy. Solo plods along undeterred.

They pass a grove of what looks like dormant aspen trees where she stops Solo and dismounts for a closer look. Bright green new growth is already starting to poke through; tiny wet sprouts shimmer in the wind. New and tender, they hold the ultimate promise of changing seasons and have pierced through winter's protective bark as nature reinvents itself once again.

She takes a deep breath and realizes that, as she had hoped, nature's renewal powers are already starting to give her new strength.

Close by, she sees the trunk of what was once a huge pine tree, its radius being more than a foot from outer bark to its center core. On the saw cut's scar, the day's dampness has caused the visible rings to appear dark, more separated from one another. She approaches the trunk, walking through wet undergrowth. She bends down and stares intently at the pattern of narrow rings, followed by wider ones and others so thin they've become almost imperceptible.

Her thoughts meld into a simple conclusion: every tree records its history through good times and bad, drought and flood and sometimes even fire and recovery. And, like the one near her cabin, some are capable of transitioning from near-death to rebirth.

She visualizes a "nurse" tree she saw in Olympic National Park's rain forest where what had been a useless, dead and fallen tree was becoming a thriving location for new and vibrant plants.

As her fingers touch the sawn trunk and she reads its past, she feels humbled and questions if psychological scars on human beings can ever be equally suitable fodder for new growth.

She remounts Solo with her spirit calmer as she continues to contemplate nature and its healing powers.

Proceeding slowly, deliberately, Solo crosses a crystal-clear stream feeding a pond, the only ripples interrupting its perfect stillness being created by the gently falling rain. Destiny follows, happily leaping through the shallow stream.

Granite Peak, rising more than 12,000 feet, provides a stunning backdrop with its lower horizontal border separating flora from its towering and barren stone cap. Below timberline, evergreen trees radiate continued hope; above it, rocky cliffs and precarious boulders warn of impending danger.

She dismounts again and sits on a large smooth boulder by the pond as Solo, his reins loosely draped over the saddle horn, munches on wet grass. Larger raindrops soon begin to create hundreds of circles on the pond.

Destiny suddenly spots a beaver swimming at one end of the pond near a log dam, its head barely out of the water and creating a small wake. She jumps into the pond and starts to swim, instantly causing the beaver to dive underwater and out of sight.

Defeated, Destiny turns back and emerges from the pond shaking her entire body and making it explode with flying water.

Suddenly, wolf howls fill the area and echo from the canyons. Before Laura can stop her, Destiny takes off, crosses back across the shallow stream feeding the pond, and, in a dead run, races up a nearby hillside.

Alarmed as she watches her disappear, Laura remounts Solo and is immediately in pursuit, yelling, "Destiny! No! Sit!"

She urges Solo to jump across the stream and gives him his head to canter up the hill. He effortlessly complies. A well-worn tire-track dirt road comes into view on the other side of the hill.

The greenery below timberline abruptly ends and the rocks above it begin. Solo is cautious, negotiating the rocky trail, where sturdy trees have suddenly given way to twisted, stunted undergrowth.

Fog begins to shroud the area. As the mist clears a bit, Laura spots what could be an abandoned log cabin a short distance away. Then she sees a dented pickup parked next to a rusted-out Jeep with a cracked windshield. She realizes the cabin may be occupied after all when she sees well-tended and healthy greenery growing in wooden planters on the porch next to two small windows, their vibrancy contrasting with the stark surroundings.

Next to the cabin she spots a small greenhouse with its glass fogged up as if it is much warmer inside. Adjoining the cabin on the opposite side is a chain-link enclosure about 100 feet by 75 feet with 10-foot-high fencing. She sees movement and can barely believe her eyes and her ears. Inside the enclosure she first sees and then begins to hear numerous wolves, pacing, barking, growling and snapping at Destiny who has skirted the enclosure to investigate, then has instantly spun around to begin her dash back, tail between her legs. Once Destiny has left the wolf compound area, the harsh howling subsides and begins to blend into several harmonies. Laura, on Solo, waits and watches Destiny running faster than she's ever run before.

The wolves have apparently alerted an older man, who appears on the cabin's porch holding a shotgun as if he's expecting to confront a two-legged intruder.

He looks to be in his late-50s, his stringy gray hair pulled back in a messy ponytail. He has a matching unkempt full gray beard completely hiding his lips. He wears a stained, long-underwear top and torn, faded jeans with thick suspenders. He is barefooted and angry.

Suddenly, she sees him raise the shotgun. He seems to have Destiny in his gun sight. But before Laura can react or call out, he fires. Hearing the shotgun blast, Destiny jumps in fright and races up and over the hill past Solo and Laura.

The shooter spots Laura as Solo shies, rears up and almost dumps her.

"What the shit you doin' up here, woman?" he yells out as his final word echoes through the canyon, "Woman? woman? woman?"

Wide-eyed and shaking, Laura waves frantically and screams back with urgency as she sees the rifle now safely pointing downward. "Sorry! Took a wrong turn! Really sorry!" She hears her own voice echo back through the rocky canyon, "Sorry, sorry, sorry…"

Immediately she yanks the reins to turn Solo around and solidly kicks his flanks. He instantly trots back down the rocky trail, following Destiny toward the beaver pond. Once out of sight of the cabin, Laura stops Solo, catches her breath, exhales loudly and wipes sweat, as well as rain, from her forehead. She repeats aloud, almost in the exact tone he used, "What the shit, indeed?"

Her ride back to Timberline Ranch is quiet and uneventful. Lost in thought for most of the way, when she finally sees the ranch's barn, she makes a firm decision not to tell Jerry about her day.

13

Cabin Fever

Back inside his cabin, Gregg's ears are still ringing with Laura's echoed response. His lips continue to form and sarcastically whisper, "Sorry! Sorry! Sorry!"

He points the shotgun's barrel at the floor and props up the gun next to a badly stained cabinet. Plopping down heavily on a metal chair, he continues to mimic her tone and attitude while shaking his head side to side and pursing his lips.

His final pronouncement, sounding oddly personal, reflects cynicism and bitterness, "Stupid bitch!"

As he spits out the words, a startled blond woman peeking out from behind the kitchen door frame, jumps visibly and then carefully inches backward on her tiptoes, disappearing into the adjoining room.

Gregg doesn't notice her. He pulls out a small cloth bag from his shirt pocket, reaches into it and removes an already rolled joint. He strikes a match and lights up, immediately sucking in the smoke and making a hissing sound through his stained teeth. He closes his eyes, leans back in the chair, holding a dirty and chipped green ceramic ashtray with a marijuana leaf painted over its entire surface. It is full of ashes along with the tiny stubs of about a dozen completely smoked joints.

Exhaled smoke creates a bluish haze in the kitchen.

14

Resting in Pieces

It's midday. For the first time in several days, blue sky abounds. Laura, on Solo, rides on River Road along the perimeter of an old graveyard, its fence long gone except for a smattering of broken and unpainted posts. Staring over the small, tilted headstones at a crumbling concrete mausoleum marked with a few engraved metal plates, she leans forward in the saddle and strains to read the one closest to her. *"Mary Snowden, beloved wife and mother. 1889-1925."*

Unable to dictate where her mind takes her, Laura returns suddenly to Texas:

She lies face down on an un-slept-in bed in the Lone Star Inn. An empty plastic syringe lays next to her, its needle retaining one unused drop. Her body is limp and she lacks energy to form words, although her lips move slightly when she tries. But she feels something taped across her mouth.

Al appears blurry to her as he wraps a sheet around her, lifts her awkwardly and carries her out to the bed of his pickup which is backed up to the motel room door.

Her head slams down on the truck's bed as he roughly pulls her by her feet towards the cab, then lifts her body into what she vaguely realizes is his metal tool box.

She passes out. Sometime later she regains consciousness but feels she can barely breathe. She feels what she recognizes as duct tape on her mouth.

She rocks from side to side as the truck travels on what she thinks is a dirt road and she hears the cold metal box grind on the truck bed. Then the truck stops. Next, she hears Al and someone else, grunting as they struggle to lift the box out of the truck bed. Instinctively, she knows she must not moan or cry out.

They carry the box a short distance and then she feels it slide onto something that sounds like concrete. A banging noise follows as if a door has closed her and the box inside. Then, silence.

Horror overtakes her.

Far-off thunder in the distant mountains brings Laura back to the moment. Startled by the sound, she looks frightened and in reflex kicks Solo who quickly canters past the cemetery. Destiny, also spooked by the noise, takes off at a full run.

"Remember, concentrate on being in the present, Laura!" she says aloud, repeating Dr. Marshall's words to her in his office when she experienced her first flashback and started to shake and cry. "Be in control of where you are and what you think. Never give Al back the power he once had. If you do, he wins. Even if he's in prison, he wins!" Marshall had firmly told her

"Take control!" she says sternly to herself, feeling the wind blowing through her hair as Solo gallops ahead. "You're in Montana on Solo. You're free!"

After the sun disappears behind the highest peaks, Laura begins to believe her own words. As a red glow fills the sky, a huge weight begins to lift from her shoulders.

15

Done In

Laura begins working in the barn, brushing Solo who munches hay while Destiny sleeps on the stall floor.

The sounds of ranch guests and employees blend with the clip-clopping of two large work horses pulling the old hay wagon. She vaguely remembers the rescheduled date and time for the hay ride, looks at her watch and walks quickly to the barn door.

Jerry, reins in his hands, drives the two horses as smiling children and adult ranch guests ride on the hay bales stacked at various levels. He sees Laura and waves.

As she smiles and waves back, she actually feels somewhat normal.

An hour later and in the cabin, she gazes out the window while drinking a glass of wine. The predicted storm has failed to develop today. Now darkness blankets the area. She sees a sky full of diamonds.

On the floor beside her, Destiny hungrily crunches a large milk bone.

Life is good.

16

Got Your Back

Laura picks up her cell phone from the kitchen table and punches in a number. Almost immediately, she begins to speak.

"Hi, Jo. Hope you're still up?"

"I am now!" she answers, sounding groggy.

"Oh, sorry! Forgot about the time change, again," Laura says immediately.

"Just kidding. I was actually still up, reading a book." Then Josephine, sounding a bit concerned, adds, "I was actually going to call you tonight."

"Let me guess, to lecture me?"

"Kinda, sorta," Josephine answers.

Laura immediately snaps back, "I knew I shouldn't have emailed you about the wolf house. Damn it! I know better! Okay, let's hear your lecture."

Without a second's hesitation, Josephine blurts out in anger, "For God's sake, Laura, stay away from there! What were you thinking? Or were you thinking at all?"

Laura stares at the cabin ceiling, frowns, walks to the couch to pick up a magazine, flipping its pages to divert her attention away from Josephine's voice.

"Sorry I ever mentioned it," Laura mumbles.

"Get real! Some idiot actually shot at your dog? You're trying to get over a husband who wanted to bury you alive! Isn't that enough excitement for one lifetime?"

Laura tosses the magazine to one side and looks serious. She feels conflicted, almost as if she's being lectured by her late mother, not an ex-roommate. But one part of her knows that Josephine is right.

After a few seconds, Laura speaks in a cynical tone, "So, would it make you feel better if I joined a convent?"

"Much better!" Josephine shoots back, "But, knowing you, you'd even dig up trouble there, too. Does the term drama queen sound familiar?"

Laura half smiles, half grimaces. "By the way, am I actually paying for this call?"

Josephine says nothing.

"Just checking," Laura says.

"The phone call, yes, but the lecture's free. As always," Josephine chuckles back.

"Gotta go, talk to you in a few days. No more time for lecturing tonight. Going to drive to the general store in Big Timber for gas and groceries. Promise I'll be careful. Bye for now."

"Are you serious? Big Timber is actually the name of a town?" Josephine laughs. "Sounds like a lumber yard. Be safe!"

17

Groceries Plus

Laura leaves Destiny asleep, picks up her wallet and keys and takes off with the convertible's top down. In 25 minutes, she's reading the green highway sign announcing Big Timber city limits and she notes its population of 1,700.

She drives into to a small general store's gravel parking lot on the town's outskirts. No other vehicles are there. She slowly pulls up to the gasoline pumps, exits her car, fills the tank and then walks inside to pay.

A large wall clock reads 8:20. A homely young man with bad acne who looks to be between 18 and his early 20s, peeks out of a back room. The glow of a television screen can be seen and obviously heavy breathing is heard coming from the audio. She hears shuffling and something small and plastic, sounding like a remote hit the floor. The television glow disappears and the audio ceases.

"Just another creep," she thinks to herself, frowning and shaking her head in disgust.

Seeing Laura, the young man, wearing a pinned-on plastic name-tag with a sloppily hand-written KEITH visible, looks a bit startled as he emerges from the back room. His haircut, mannerisms and speech make him a full-fledged mountain weirdo to her. When he speaks, she realizes he's probably harmless.

"Can I help you find anything, Miss?" he pants, out of breath.

Laura avoids eye contact. She sounds business-like, not haughty.

"I owe you for gas and I need some groceries, too," she says as she gathers a few items and places them in a small wire basket.

Keith checks the gasoline tab on the small digital readout and punches in numbers on a cash register. Laura approaches the check-out counter holding a credit card. Keith ogles her.

"It's $20.72 for the gas. Groceries on yer card, too?"

She nods.

He rings up the items. She hands him the card, looking away and trying not to think about the video.

"You stayin' around here?" Keith asks.

Laura, reluctant to reveal much, mumbles, "Up near the lake."

"Oh, so you're the one."

She looks surprised and feels instantly uncomfortable, wondering if he knows about her background, the trial, her history. She doesn't like the paranoid feelings closing in but can't seem to shake them.

"Heard of me?" she asks hesitantly.

"Jerry at Timberline Ranch is my cousin. Said he'd met you."

Somewhat relieved, she exhales and smiles ever-so-slightly, "Small town, I guess."

As Keith gives her the credit-card chit to sign, he reads her name off her card. He stares hungrily at her as she signs.

"So, er, Laura, how ya like it up here? Heard you went ridin'," he says, grinning.

She is barely civil now and coldly responds, "Like it fine so far."

"See any big-horn sheep up there yet?

"Not yet."

"Watch out for that ol' guy back up behind the ranch property," Keith, says, sounding protective.

Her interest is piqued and she loosens up a bit. The reporter in her resurfaces and she realizes Keith might have some information she wants. She realizes there is a story here, something she's more than curious about. Nerdy creepy Keith could be a good source if she plays her cards right.

Her tone changes and she becomes more friendly, "Really? Tell me about him."

As Keith bags her groceries, his demeanor suddenly changes, too. He swells with self-importance and his tone shifts as well.

Despite being the only two in the store, he leans forward as if he's giving her the inside scoop, and he begins whispering out of the side of his mouth, "First off, they got lots of dogs up there. Heard they was vicious. We think the guy's high on somethin', too. Acts real weird sometimes when he come in the store."

She tempts him with a few details in a near-whisper, "I rode up there today."

Shocked, Keith fires back, "Better not do that! It's against the ranch rules for dudes, er, people to go outside the property line, above timberline, ya know. Jerry'll be pissed."

She leans in towards Keith who seems to love the closeness, "Do me a favor, um, Keith? Don't mention that to Jerry. I got a bit lost. Wasn't supposed to ride off ranch property. Won't happen again. It will be our secret, okay?"

His lips form a sly, confidential grin.

As she picks up her grocery bag and starts to leave, Keith seems desperate to talk and he tries to work a deal.

"Promise I'll keep it to myself, er, if you'll have coffee with me after I close up. I can tell you some more about them hippies."

He glances at the clock.

"Just 10 more minutes. We can go across to Crystal's."

She considers it for a moment. The reporter in her hears the word hippies for the second time recently and she knows she's going to agree. She hears Dr. Marshall suggesting, "Do what you're afraid to do." She wants to walk away to go back to the cabin, as Josephine suggested and not lead a drama-queen life, but then she sniffs a unique story. She seems unaware that her own troubles have suddenly taken a back seat to her curiosity about the wolf man.

"Okay, Keith," she hears herself saying. "I guess I can meet you at Crystal's, but for coffee only. Period."

Keith looks like his ship has just come in. He grins, tries to contain himself, and says, "Period! I'll meet you across the road."

18

Clouded Crystal

Laura walks out of the store to her car, popping the trunk and placing her items inside. She looks over at the cafe on the opposite side of the highway. Two big rigs are parked in the lot in front of the small, one-story, bright-yellow stucco cafe.

The flashing red neon sign on its roof demands passersby to stop and, "EAT! EAT! EAT!" in stark contrast to the Alpine backdrop where royal velvet mountains seem painted on the inky sky, subtly offering serenity, free to one and all.

"This should be interesting," she thinks to herself with no hint of nervousness or apprehension as she walks across the two-lane road, stops and climbs the weathered wooden stairs to the cafe, its screen door askew.

Once inside, she notices how run-down and outdated the place is. If she were writing an article, she would describe it as "beyond retro." Despite the late hour, two heavy-set truckers in their 60s eat bacon and eggs and slurp coffee. They check out Laura as she enters, smile at each other and exchange a couple of remarks. The rest of the cafe is empty.

Crystal's has a dozen or so heavily worn and cracked red-vinyl booths with rarely seen individual jukebox units. Near the kitchen, a counter area with six stools awaits customers.

Crystal herself, her name sparkling from her sequined nametag, tops off the truckers' coffee and eyes Laura suspiciously as she walks quickly past the "seat yourself" sign to the last booth in the back next to a large picture window. Laura feels drawn to the booth, its window framing a distant pasture softly illuminated by moonlight.

Crystal's teased platinum hair falls sporadically from a failed French twist, her black roots crying out for peroxide. Heavily made up and wearing outdated oversized pink-frame glasses, she walks as if her feet hurt.

"Hey, what can I get for ya, hon?" Crystal calls out to her from near the truckers' booth, grinding her gum and looking sideways at Laura.

"Cup of decaf, please."

"Sorry, Hon. Just finished the last pot. Too late to brew more. Closin' soon. High test okay?"

"Just hot chocolate. Thanks."

Crystal sighs heavily, frowns but says nothing as she snaps her gum and trudges into the kitchen. Laura notices her demeanor and wonders if she has mistakenly requested rare French Champagne.

Returning with a small envelope of instant cocoa and a mug of steaming water, Crystal realizes she has forgotten a spoon and napkin and snatches one of each from a nearby table stacked with dirty dishes. She off-handedly tosses them down in front of Laura who picks up the napkin, and, pursing her lips, examines it to see if it has been used before, then polishes the spoon with it as Crystal watches.

Keith suddenly bursts through the front door. It bangs shut. He's slicked back his hair and closed the snap button at the collar of his western shirt.

To Laura, he looks even more nerdy than before and the acne on his forehead is much more noticeable and bumpy. She doubts she's made the right choice to meet him and realizes her curiosity about the wolf man may have gotten the best of her judgment.

As he heads for Laura's booth, Crystal holds back a grin, her hand over her mouth, as she tries to catch his eye. He's too enamored to notice as he rushes to the back.

"Thanks for stayin'," he says loudly, focusing on Laura. "I was afraid ya might just leave."

"No. I'm anxious to hear the details on those hippies," she says quietly.

He slides into the booth and sits across from her, seeming to gain self-assurance after hearing her comment. He leans forward and immediately starts to speak lowly, confidentially, without any transition from their previous conversation.

"Well, they're really weird, that's fer sure. Livin' up there above the trees an' all. Only rocks grows up there," he says, smiling and looking proud of his humorous remark.

She smiles back as if on cue.

"Only seen the wife a couple times. The husband does all their shoppin'. She rides along sometimes but always stays in their pickup."

Laura begins taking mental notes. She has learned not to interrupt someone giving her sought-after facts.

"They don't hardly ever get no mail. Have a mailbox inside our store like ever'body who lives way up there does," he says. "No mail delivery round here, neither. And ever' thing that's mailed to them goes to Los Lobos Cabin. That's what they call their place; it's named after that old rock group."

Keith watches Laura to see her reaction to his knowledge of rock-music history.

She remains silent as she mentally translates the Spanish words into, *"The Wolves' Cabin"*.

Keith continues, "But, he sure buys a whole lot of booze. My boss says he's one of our best customers ever. Buys beer, cases of it."

Crystal arrives at the booth with Keith's coffee and six small plastic cream containers without his asking, then she shuffles away. Keith rips each one open and splashes the liquid into his coffee, turning it to light tan and almost causing the cup to overflow. He methodically adds three full teaspoons of sugar.

"How do they make their money?" Laura asks, watching him stir the concoction.

As he talks, Laura concentrates on continuing to look interested, almost as if enthralled.

It works.

Keith answers excitedly, "Don't rightly know. Checks come from some bank in Alaska ever' month. He cashes them here in Big

Timber sometimes. But, sometimes he don't even pick 'em up fer weeks. One time the boss found a deposit slip he dropped by mistake and told Jerry and me he had over a hundred grand in the bank in Big Timber."

Laura's eyes widen as if she has never heard of such a thing.

"Anyways, I got to talkin' to Gregg, that's the husband. Told me they used to live way the heck up in north Alaska. Told me they got lots of dogs. Huskies."

"Really!" she states, keeping direct eye contact with him and not revealing anything she knows.

"Yep, he buys a dozen cases of frozen chicken and turkey parts ever' couple months. Gotta have them brought in special by a refrigerated truck. Costs him a pretty penny. They must have one hell of a big freezer!"

The truckers stand to leave. They comment quietly to Crystal as she adds up their tab and takes their money. The three look back at the odd couple and all have a short chuckle.

Laura sees the threesome smiling and asks Keith, looking into his eyes, "I just wonder if that Gregg guy is off his rocker or what? What do you think, Keith?"

Keith, taken aback by her mentioning his own name and giving him sudden attention, gazes at Laura. He seems at a loss for words. He does not respond. He quickly slurps some coffee.

She sips the last of her hot chocolate and prepares to leave.

Keith, desperate for their meeting to continue, can't seem to think of anything to encourage her to stay.

"Ya sure do ask a lot of questions," he says suddenly, shaking his head.

Laura stands, picks up her bill and doesn't comment.

"Tell ya what, I'll try to find out more from Duane. He's our sheriff. I got his home number. He comes to the general store lots of times during the day, too."

Laura sees Crystal's expression as she stands by the front door checking her watch. She isn't actually tapping her foot but Laura can feel her urgency and disapproval and starts for the door, money in hand, including tip.

Keith, still trying to prolong this "date," also stands, leaves a couple of dollars and some change on the table.

"How 'bout you meetin' me here again tomorrow night? There's a dance at Timberline's hall at 8," Keith blurts out as she turns her back on him and proceeds toward the door, handing the check and money to Crystal.

"Duane'll be here too," Keith quickly adds.

Laura considers, looks back at Keith and exhales, "I don't think I can do that, Keith."

Keith pleads. "Ah, come on. Just think about it?"

Laura waves and dismisses him in one gesture, "Night, Keith," she says as Crystal smirks and notices Keith's defeated expression as the door closes in his face.

19

Ridin' High

Laura rides Solo on the loop trail. Destiny trots alongside. The sun is directly overhead. They stop by a stream where she dismounts and ties Solo loosely to a small aspen tree so he can comfortably graze. She takes a sandwich from her saddlebag, along with a soda and a small plastic bag. She opens the bag and tosses Destiny a couple of milk bones.

Lying back on the soft grass and stretching out next to the stream, she takes a bite of her sandwich and stares up at the picture-perfect day. Solo munches on the grasses lining the stream, stopping to take an occasional long drink between bites. Sunlight bathes them.

Suddenly, gunshots erupt in the distance. Both Laura and Destiny are startled and jump to their feet. Solo shies and pulls the reins loose from the tree where he was tied. He starts to trot away. Laura runs after him and grabs the reins.

A woman who looks to be in her late-30s, whose leathery face has seen lots of high-altitude sun, bounces toward them driving the old Jeep that Laura saw preiously. She splashes it through the shallow creek, spraying water where Laura has just been lying.

The Jeep tears past Laura and Solo, the woman not seeming to notice them. One of her eyes is swollen almost shut and she cocks her head to one side to see through the cracked windshield, barely staying within the tire tracks.

Seeing the woman sobbing, Laura yells out, "Good God!"

As the Jeep disappears down the trail, Laura quickly gathers her soda, her lunch bag and the remainder of her sandwich, stuffs them into the saddle bag and remounts Solo. She heads uphill toward Los Lobos Cabin.

Destiny follows.

Tying Solo to a tree at the base of a small rise, Laura hikes up the hill to get a view of the cabin. She retrieves the squashed sandwich and feeds it to Destiny in small bites to keep her quiet. Then, lying flat, Laura peeks through some foot-high weeds and recognizes who she now knows to be Gregg on the cabin porch. He is cleaning his rifle.

The wolves are restless, pacing in the adjoining compound. He yells angrily to them in a foreign language, "Nepengyaq!" It has a strange guttural sound.

Then, without warning, he loads the rifle and fires again into the air. Laura jumps, then inches backward down the hill with Destiny leading the way. She remounts Solo and turns him around to beat a hasty retreat. Soda drips from the wet saddle bag.

On the ride back to the ranch, she remembers Josephine's warning and feels ashamed to have let her curiosity get the better of her. Her friend's description of her as a "drama queen" keeps returning to her mind. Entering the ranch property, she considers whether she is indeed sometimes a magnet for trouble. The fleeting idea that she may have made some bad choices today quickly leaves her consciousness.

Before mid-afternoon, she is driving her car with Destiny beside her, heading away from Timberline Ranch and toward her cabin. Her digital watch reads 3:45.

In a shorter time than she realizes, it is pitch black out and Laura's car, sans Destiny, sits in front of the general store.

She finds herself in the back booth at Crystal's sipping coffee with Keith next to the picture window. Laura had gone to buy treats and milk bones for Destiny just as Keith was closing early to go to the Timberline dance, and, in no time, allowed herself be talked into meeting Duane and Keith at the cafe.

Keith appears eager to impress her. She looks uncomfortable with him, checking around to see if anyone is watching. She relaxes slightly when she sees two cowboys walk to the register to pay and head for the door, leaving no other customers to stare at her.

She sees Duane coming in at the same time, the men exchanging nods. Duane removes his hat.

Laura estimates he is in his early 40s. She immediately notices he is well-built and handsome in his freshly pressed deputy sheriff's uniform. He confidently strides directly to the back booth and without smiling at or greeting Keith extends his hand to Laura. They briefly lock eyes as he sits down and begins to speak immediately.

"Hello, you must be Laura. I'm Duane," he says in a no-nonsense tone. "Keith told me you'd been up to the hippies' place above Timberline Ranch. We don't know much about them. About all we know is that they own a bunch of Huskies from Alaska."

Duane seems to get right to the task at hand with no preliminaries, no socializing. Laura hears his comments and nods her head.

She has always felt safe with police officers, remembering positive interactions as a reporter in Texas. She was taken along on several "sting" operations, being trusted not to blow their cover as the Laredo police made a few drug busts on the streets of that famous border town. Because she always wrote positive follow-up articles about law enforcement, they trusted her. Few other journalists enjoyed that closeness.

Sounding like a prosecutor in criminal court, Duane continues his examination, unsmiling, "Did you get to talk to either of the residents?"

Laura stops, waits for a dramatic two seconds before responding, "No. But the guy shot at my dog a couple days ago!"

Duane seems shocked at her words, his eyes widening, "You're serious?"

"I didn't share that with Keith," she says.

Keith looks instantly chagrined.

"And, by the way, they have a bunch of wolves, not dogs!" she states with an air of confidence. Looking over at Keith, she adds, "They call their place Los Lobos Cabin, too, right?"

Keith nods.

"That's Spanish for the wolves' cabin," she adds. "Probably not named for the old rock group, from what I saw."

Both Keith and Duane immediately look at one another and back at Laura.

Keith frowns. "She's right. That's how their mail comes, addressed to Los Lobos Cabin!"

Duane shakes his head and narrows his eyes with skepticism.

She ignores his suspicions and adds without reservation, "Most, if not all, of the animals are definitely wolves with maybe a couple hybrid-wolf mixes thrown in. I only had a quick glimpse of them."

Duane, frowning, continues to be dubious, "Huskies is what the owner told people around here. Sure you didn't mistake them for wolves?"

She counters with a steady tone of confident authority. She holds her head higher than normal and announces, "I definitely know a wolf from a Husky. Used to volunteer in an animal rescue center."

"Well, it's not against the law to have pet wolves either, so whatever they do up there is fine with me," Duane says with equal authority.

She snaps back, "Even shooting at my dog?"

Their game of one-upmanship ends in a draw.

Duane says nothing. He stares at Laura's hands. He sees they're without rings. She notices him staring and takes a quick look at his ring-less fingers, too.

"Then something else weird happened again today," she says, notching up the conversation again.

Leaning forward, Keith seems more interested in what she's saying than Duane who has a definite smirk on his face. Laura doesn't immediately back up her comment. She stares at Duane; Keith stares at her. It's a stand-off as to who will break the silence.

Finally Duane gives in, "So, tell me what was weird?"

"I was riding Vince's horse, Solo, near their place when I heard gunshots. Again."

She seems to have captured Duane's attention now. He's listening intently.

"Then, a woman, I guess it's his wife, drove an old trashed Jeep really fast as if she was escaping something or someone, down the hill, sobbing. Looked like she had a black eye, too."

Duane frowns and returns to his legalistic tone. "Hmmm. You realize, though, it's not against the law to discharge a firearm up there. He might have just been doing target practice. And, as for her black eye, who knows how that happened?"

Laura becomes angry and spits out her words, her eyes bulging and her voice rising, "So you immediately think there's probably a good explanation for her black eye? Well, I do, too. Her lousy rotten husband punched her! That's what happened! It's good he didn't kill her!"

Duane blinks in surprise and asks her, "Wow! Where did that come from?"

Keith's head goes back and forth between the two of them as if he's watching a tennis match.

She ignores Duane's personal observation disguised as a question and continues, "I'm telling you those shots came from their cabin! So, anyway, I rode up and stayed out of sight. That's when I saw the freaking weirdo holding his rifle. He shot it again into the air."

Duane starts to grin slightly at her description, "Could have gone off accidentally when he was cleaning it or maybe he was just target shooting!"

She takes a deep breath and exhales, "You may be right. I used to be a newspaper reporter. Maybe I've just seen one too many wackos!"

Duane smiles again. "That makes two of us! As a deputy sheriff, I've probably seen more than my share of them too. I'm probably downright twisted by now. Sorry I sounded so rude. Can we start over?"

Laura looks down and says quietly, "We're both possibly a bit jaded, given our professions. Let's begin again." She pauses and smiles, "Hello, officer."

They both visibly relax.

Keith, nonplused, looks as if he realizes he's now part of the background, kind of like the jukebox music.

Looking sincere and sounding almost philosophical, Duane continues, "One thing ya learn. Lots of folks move way up here to escape from something. Pollution, crime, big cities—but most often to escape their own pasts. Some just want to wipe their slate clean.

We find the higher they move up the mountain, the more they have to escape from."

He takes a sip of coffee.

Laura nods knowingly.

Duane adds with another partial grin, "By the way, I used to be a cop down below in Bozeman before I moved way up here, if that tells you anything."

Still trying to get back into the conversation, Keith looks at Laura and quickly adds, "And remember, these here's called the Crazy Mountains! I ain't kiddin' ya neither. That's their real name."

Keith gets no reaction from either Duane or Laura who have locked eyes as if they have discovered they might have a connection after all.

Shrugging, Keith puts a coin into the jukebox and pushes buttons. He tries to shift their attention, "I really like Shania singin' this one. It's my favorite. It's…"

Duane and Laura smile, tolerate him, and return to their conversation, each looking deeply into the other's eyes, not as if totally attracted to one another but as if pleasantly surprised at having anything at all in common.

"Where were you a reporter?" Duane asks with new interest.

"In Texas, along the Mexican border."

Duane grimaces, "God! That's kind of a dangerous location now days with the drug cartels and all. Did you ever go into Mexico?"

Laura nods, answering in her own code that she knows Duane can't break, "For sure it was dangerous! I'll tell you about it someday if you're interested."

Duane tries to read her face and comment but skips to the next subject, "So, how'd you end up here?"

"It's all part of the same long story," she answers, looking as if the subject is not up for further discussion.

The moment is interrupted when Crystal shows up with the coffee pot and gives Duane a "What _are_ you thinking?" look, as she refills his empty cup, then glances at Laura who doesn't notice Crystal's disapproving stares.

Crystal shuffles off, shaking her head noticeably. Duane rolls his eyes in her direction but there is no response. Trying to take the hint from Laura to change the subject, Duane asks a follow-up question and then wishes he hadn't, "You married?"

Laura answers matter-of-factly, almost coldly, "Not any more. That's also part of the whole long story."

As he hears her words, a sad look sweeps over Duane's face and he adds, "Not married either, anymore. A whole 'nother story, too. We'll have to compare notes."

They give each other knowing glances.

Keith who has tired of the scene and has been looking for a place to jump in, suddenly bellows in an almost gleeful tone, totally inappropriate for the moment, "Been there, done that, eh?"

He smiles at them both as if congratulating himself on his cleverness. Duane and Laura stare at each other silently. In the silence, Keith fidgets and asks, "You two gonna talk all night or are we gonna drive up to the dance? It's already started. Crystal's closing in 10 minutes!"

Laura looks at Duane for direction. He recognizes her indecision and says, "I have to go to keep an eye on things, anyway. Want to just meet us there? Follow me and then you can play it by ear."

Laura nods and stands, getting money from her wallet and placing it on the check Crystal has left her, "I'll probably just watch. Haven't danced in quite a while. I do know how to get to Timberline Ranch, though. Do it on a regular basis. Meet you there."

Duane retrieves her money and hands it back to her, "Coffee's on me; besides, I owe Keith."

As they pass Crystal, who is next to the cash register, Duane leaves the bill and money, avoiding eye contact or comments from her.

20

Dancing By Heart

Dim lights cast an amber glow over the large knotty-pine room. Dancers of all ages sway to the music, a slow romantic piece sung by a spotlighted male singer in western garb, accompanied by a slightly off-key, four-piece, rag-tag band.

Cigarette smoke hangs over the room.

Laura, Keith and Duane sit at a small round table, looking like an odd threesome. Laura and Keith hold untouched glasses of draft beer. Duane drinks Coke from a can. Each of them seems to be elsewhere.

One song ends; another begins.

Somewhat hesitantly, Duane stands and extends his hand toward Laura's. She pulls her hand back into her lap and shakes her head. He keeps his hand out. She slowly takes it, but doesn't stand. He waits a second and then gently pulls her to her feet and onto the dance floor.

Keith watches with envy, his elbows on the table, his face in his hands as he mouths, "Shit!"

Neither Duane nor Laura speaks for a while. They both seem to be in their own worlds. Their feet remember what to do. They dance from memory.

Laura finally breaks the ice. "This feels pretty weird after almost two years of marriage."

Duane looks into her eyes, nods sympathetically. He is not hold-ing her close but he is holding her. She seems comfortable tonight talking to him about her personal feelings.

"Try eight!" Duane says softly, not seeming to address her directly but rather talking to himself.

They continue to dance for a while in silence. Then Duane speaks as if Laura and he were continuing a conversation. With no prelude, he says, "Thought we had a good life 'til she just up and left with our next-door neighbor."

Laura shakes her head and looks into his eyes. "Sad. You didn't have a clue?"

"Nope. Guess I was the last person in Bozeman to know."

Taking a deep breath, he blurts out the scenario, "I worked the night shift, patrolling the streets, and she worked days at the hospi-tal. Turns out she and our neighbor were keeping each other warm on those chilly Montana nights while his wife worked until 6 a.m. at Denny's. This went on for two years before I came home sick one night and found him in my bed. They took off together right after that."

Looking at Duane with empathy, she shakes her head.

"How 'bout you?" he asks.

Still playing it close to the vest, she answers without elaboration, "I had lots of clues. I just chose to ignore them."

"So, what's the story?"

"You'd never believe it. Some day when you have a couple hours to kill, I'll tell you. In the meantime, I'm trying to forget," she says, sighing. "Wonder if I'll ever be able to?" she adds, sounding as if she's making more of a statement than asking a question.

Laura stares over his shoulder. The lights are low, the dancers silhouetted in the smoke. No faces are discernible. She begins to feel invisible too.

"Know what ya mean. Guess we're both a bit gun shy," Duane says softly.

They continue to dance to their own music.

21

Hey Dude

Laura and Jerry work in the barn brushing horses and carrying hay and oats to the feed bins as the sun comes up. Destiny sniffs around at the stalls, annoying the horses.

Jerry stops and leans on one of the stall doors and asks, "Question. Would you consider taking a group of dudes on the loop trail today?"

She first looks surprised, then pleased. "Me? Sure. Guess I could handle that. Done the loop a dozen or so times now on Solo. What's up?"

"Vince needs me to go into Bozeman to buy parts for our freezer. Damned thing goes out 'bout once a month. Be much obliged if you'd help us out. Vince says he'll take a few bucks off your horse rental for that and all you're doin' around here to help out. He needs you to sign this and give your Social Security number, too. You'd be a sorta employee, the lawyer told Vince, but your pay is just the discount on the horse rent," Jerry says, handing her a sheet of paper and a pen. She complies without reading the agreement and gives the paper and pen back to him.

"Okay. Fine. I'll go home, do a few things and be back in time for the late morning ride at eleven. Anything special you want them to see?"

"Big-horn sheep if you can find any. That's a tall order, though. They're usually above timberline on them rocky areas."

A few hours later, Laura is back at the corral. Looking every bit the trail guide, she's wearing jeans, a plaid shirt, and a cowboy hat and boots. A canteen is strapped to her belt. Jerry attaches a first-aid kit to the back of Solo's saddle and fills the large saddle bags with food and drinks.

A middle-aged man walks toward him and says, "Hey, Jerry, is this cute young thing our trail guide for the afternoon? If so, she's way better looking than you, bro."

She smiles at him.

Jerry answers, "Don't know if that's much of a compliment, Laura, most ever'body is."

Guests of all ages dressed in cowboy garb start to gather at the corral while Jerry and some of the ranch staff help them onto their horses.

As Laura adjusts Solo's cinch, she sees a man in his 30s, watching guests mount horses. He seems to want to join the group, then turns and walks away. A lone horse remains tied to the fence as the group forms a single line with their horses and follows Laura to the trail head.

An hour passes as Laura slowly leads the guests along the loop trail. As they ride, she points out deer, birds and various plants. Destiny follows happily as they wind their way up and up, close to timberline.

Laura decides to add a bit of local color to her trail presentation and stops to point to the distinct line on the opposing mountainside.

"As you folks can see the few plants that do exist just above timberline are twisted, gnarled and not symmetrical. In other words, they're not quite normal."

The guests use their binoculars and some begin to comment while zeroing in, "Yeah, I can see that. Some wildflowers are barely visible at all," one man says.

She adds, "I've been told the people themselves who live up beyond timberline are pretty different too. Some might even be a bit twisted as well."

Then a woman who introduced herself earlier to Laura as Sue Brice, a physician from Boston, comments in an academic tone, "What fascinates me is how the altitude may affect drug use, even some over-the-counter drugs work differently in the high altitudes. Recent research I read indicates that marijuana may even double its effects."

"The higher you go, the higher you get?" one of the younger men calls out.

The doctor smiles, "I wouldn't know personally but that's what some tests have found. The effect of alcohol is also somewhat enhanced."

"So people who live up there above timberline could accurately be called cheap drunks, eh?" Laura laughs.

"Are you serious? Do people actually live way up there? It looks God-forsaken to me!" an older man says.

"A few do live up there, according to locals I have spoken to," Laura replies. "I've heard they're mostly hippies and hermits."

Dr. Brice adds, "When I get back home I'm going to do some online research to see if, just like the trees and ground cover striving to live above timberline, that only the hardiest of humans can survive up there, or as Laura says, do they become abnormal, too."

The doctor does not seem to be joking or only vaguely interested.

Laura looks intrigued by the doctor's comments and observations and listens carefully, knowing if she were to write a feature article about people choosing to live above timberline, the doctor's quotes could be used to provide credibility.

"It is also more difficult to breathe at the highest altitudes where oxygen is scarce, but my medical background tells me that the effort itself will actually make your lungs stronger and give you more lung capacity, like professional athletes who choose to go to Mexico City or Denver to train."

Laura considers what she has just heard and has one final comment before moving on with the ride, "So let's see now, doctor, people living above timberline can smoke less pot and get the same effect, drink less booze and feel just as good, and take deep breaths and have a bigger lung capacity. Some would ask, what's not to like?"

The doctor smiles but quickly counters with something that sounds like it's straight from a medical textbook, "Well, how about the inability to fully focus or concentrate, frequent nausea and light-headedness, with lethargy and dizziness thrown in just for starters?"

The doctor, the dudes and Laura all laugh heartily.

22

Big Sky High

Laura gently kicks Solo to begin walking again and the other horses and riders follow.

"Let's move on now and stop at the pond up ahead."

As they come within a few feet of the beaver pond and begin to circle it, the horses and riders are reflected in its perfectly still water. Many immediately notice the unique beauty Laura has come to almost take for granted. They stop for photos using their phones or small cameras.

Soon the group arrives at a rest area for horses where a weathered wooden railing stands ready to secure them.

Laura signals for everyone to stop and dismount.

"We'll have our lunch now," she says, retrieving drinks and food from Solo's saddlebags.

After placing bright plastic tablecloths and the picnic lunches on the grass, Laura calls, "Soup's on! Enjoy yourselves, folks."

She returns to Solo's side to get bags of chips, placing them at the center of each tablecloth. Some of the guests immediately come forward, pick up their food and return to the pond's edge to sit. Others take their time to absorb the scenery and lead their horses to drink from the pond or graze on the grass.

Suddenly, ear-splitting screams echo through the canyon. Guests who were stretched out on the grass jump to their feet.

"Leave me alone! Get away from me!" they hear a woman shout in fear.

"Fine! Fine! Get out, you crazy bitch!" a man yells back.

Guests look at one another in shock, then to Laura for an explanation. She is uncomfortable but tries to make light of it.

Then the sound of a vehicle peeling out nearby fills the air. In just a few seconds, dust flies as the fast-moving Jeep heads directly toward the pond.

The guests look concerned until Laura speaks, "No worries, folks. Sorry. Guess those hippies are having another domestic spat. They live over that hill. I heard them once before."

"Trouble in paradise?" a woman asks rhetorically.

In less than a minute, the Jeep speeds down the dusty tire-track road near the pond. The blonde woman is driving again and looks so enraged that she doesn't seem to see anyone or anything.

Laura shrugs her shoulders when the group looks back again to her for further explanation. The Jeep splashes through the creek and travels on toward Timberline Ranch leaving its dusty wake to settle over the pond, the people and the food.

23

Calling the Cops

It's getting dark. Laura is on the phone in the middle of a conversation.

"Anyway, this is the second time I know of that she's taken off. Guess their relationship is stormy."

"Hmmm. Sounds more like it's volcanic! My advice is to stay away from weirdos," Duane answers.

He has his feet propped up on his desk and is reclined in his chair at the sheriff's sub-station office. "Want to discuss it further over a hamburger at Crystal's?"

"I'm pretty tired. Took all afternoon to supervise the ride for the dudes at the ranch, plus out of nervousness I ate more than the usual amount of the food we brought along. Helped with all the horses afterwards, too. Thanks, though."

Resigned to just talking on the phone, Duane begins sounding more philosophical and investigative, "No problem. Back to the Jeep woman, all I can say is, it happens. At least she gets mad, storms out, comes back. Karen just left me a note. We never even had cross words. But, I'm trying to let all that go." Duane pauses briefly, and then adds in a softer tone, "Now."

Laura gets the message and sighs a understanding, "Uh, huh."

Without taking another breath, Duane asks, "Say, how 'bout going into Livingston for dinner and a movie tomorrow night? I'm off at 5."

Laura considers for a moment. She takes a deep breath and starts to decline his offer. She first sounds uncertain, then conflicted, and finally hesitantly agrees with a proviso, "Well, um, okay. Mind if we take my convertible? I have trouble riding in anything closed in."

"Whatever you want works for me," he says as he stands, slightly grins at himself in the mirror on the back of the office door and puts on his hat. "See ya tomorrow."

24

Picture This

Duane and Laura sit stiffly, watching as the large movie screen lights up their faces. They both seem preoccupied. Duane awkwardly sneaks his arm around her, looking a bit like a teenager on his first date.

She edges slightly away, bites her lower lip and appears uncomfortable.

He notices, squeezes her shoulder and removes his arm. She smiles at him as if to thank him for understanding. When the movie ends and they stand to exit, Laura slips her hand in his. He pulls her closer and smiles.

They drive back in silence, listening to music, each in a separate bubble. When they arrive at her cabin, Duane walks her up the stairs. They stop on the porch. Neither speaks for a couple of seconds.

"I had a good time tonight," he says, looking at her and smiling slightly. "Not the best movie I've seen but good company just the same."

"I agree," she says back. "Thanks for being so patient. Even getting damp in my convertible with the top down."

"What's a little sprinkle among friends?" he says.

She leans up against the door and seems to speak from her heart and from a new perspective, "I've been a bit of a hermit for a few weeks. Dogs and horses are my only companions."

"Plus a few dudes?" Duane adds.

She smiles, "Yeah, plus a few dudes. But I really didn't talk to them much. Trail guide. That's me. At least I'm employed, more or less."

"I know Vince appreciates you helping out."

"I gotta find a real job one of these days. Kind of miss reporting and writing."

"Hasn't been a newspaper in this place for years, "Duane says. "Maybe you should start one."

"Gotta have something to write about first. Maybe I could do a freelance piece for a magazine about people who hide in the mountains."

"Would that be autobiographical?" Duane smirks.

She gives him a slight punch on the upper arm and a cynical, "Yeah, right!"

"Anyway, thanks for tonight. Enjoyed our time together," Duane says, starting back down the stairs to where his patrol car is waiting.

"Thanks. I had fun, too. Thought I had forgotten how."

Destiny is heard racing around inside the cabin, barking.

As Laura opens the screen door, she stops. Duane comes back. He gently puts his arm around her, pulls her close and gives her a quick, tender kiss on the lips.

She feels somewhat conflicted but says, looking directly into his eyes, "Thanks."

25

Crystal's Ball

The cafe is empty except for Duane and Crystal who sit in one of the front booths hunched over their coffee cups. She seems eager to extract information from him. But, he remains tight-lipped.

"So, Mister Sheriff's Captain Duane, I hear you and the new gal are an item."

Duane smiles a bit, but is not revealing information.

"And I hear, that you, Miss Crystal's Cafe owner, have an overactive imagination."

"Well, I know what I see and I know what Keith says."

Duane fires back, "Oh, now I get it, and we all know Keith has an overactive something or other. Now he's a gossip reporter for inquiring minds?"

Crystal cackles loud and long, slapping Duane playfully on the wrist.

Just then, Duane's cell phone goes off. He checks it, takes one last sip of coffee and stands. He heads out the door, not looking back at Crystal.

She shakes her head as if it's not the first time this has happened.

"Saved by the bell, ya lucky bastard!" she hollers out the door. "Plus you just ripped me off for coffee! Again!"

26

Sheep's Clothing

Gregg and Evie sit next to each other on a weathered wooden bench on their cabin's porch. She seems distracted and gazes across the canyon at the huge granite mountain opposite them.

Gregg looks at her, reaches over and begins to examine her injured eye. "Can't believe Yupik did that! Broke the skin and everything."

He sounds concerned.

She looks back at him with contempt, "Right!" Her tone is icy.

"Maybe we should put her down since now she can't be trusted anymore—too unpredictable. She might have killed you if I hadn't heard you scream and come running," he says with scorn.

Evie immediately stands, walks a few feet away from him, and holds onto the porch railing, still looking out at the mountain, her back to Gregg. Under her breath she whispers almost imperceptibly, "Maybe we should just put you down, too, since you can't be trusted, either."

Then, in a normal tone, she says, "She just didn't see me coming into her den. I surprised her and she was nursing her cubs. She would have done the same to you, Gregg."

"Nope. She wouldn't have attacked me because I wouldn't have put myself in that stupid position! I know better and so do you!" he snaps back at her as he lights up a joint. "This has happened too many times, Evie, and you always blame yourself, never them. Never, ever the wolves!"

Evie, still not looking at Gregg, continues to debate, "Remember when Tundra bit you on the butt, big time? Broke the skin then, too."

He doesn't respond.

"You didn't talk about killing her then. You understood wolves. But that was before," Evie says, almost shouting.

"Before what?" he demands, looking angry and staring at her with cold eyes.

"Before you became a drunk and a pot head! Before was when you made good decisions."

He screams back, "Oh, I thought *before* was when you brushed your teeth, wore clean clothes, washed your hair! *Before* was when you took a bath and cleaned up the wolf shit in the house! That was *before*, too!"

He stands, picks up his beer and stomps back into the cabin.

Evie returns to the cabin and takes down a Ziploc bag from the top shelf over the stove in the kitchen. It's tucked into an almost invisible space where Gregg would never discover it. She looks around to be sure he isn't watching. She sees his back toward her and predicts he's heading to the couch to watch television, his regular routine.

She slowly opens the bag and carefully takes out several dried leaves of all colors—deep red, rust, gold, bright yellow, orange and even a small green one. She places each one on part of a large open napkin, facing them so that no one could see them but her. She slowly examines each one as if she remembers when and where she collected it.

After a few minutes, she sighs and seems calmer. Then she carefully replaces each one, as if it's a secret treasure, back into the bag, zips it closed and puts it into its hiding place.

27

Past As Prologue

Sitting on the couch in her cabin, Duane and Laura sip wine and look at newspaper clippings about Al's trial. Dinner dishes remain on the kitchen table. There is a small fire in the fireplace. Rain falls gently outside. Duane finishes reading an article and puts it back into the box on the hearth. He takes a deep breath and begins to flip through three or four pages in the wedding album she has pulled from under the couch. He settles on the one photo of Laura and Al standing at the church altar. He stares sadly and asks rhetorically, "Who could have ever predicted?"

She stares into the fire. "Now you understand about the convertible top?"

He reaches over and pats her head gently and runs his fingers through her hair affectionately, "Yep. I do. Now."

He places the album back into her hands and says, "God! You both look so, um, innocent and hopeful at your wedding."

"Told you it was a long, unbelievable story!"

"So he's in federal prison for at least 25 years for kidnapping and attempted murder? Seems he got off easy."

She nods.

"When did you find out he'd had a criminal record as a juvenile and a history of violence?"

Laura smirks, "I had some clues, looking back, but it all came out in the trial. Al told me he had been in trouble as a kid, but reassured me that it was all a big mistake. He was raised in several foster homes, never saw his parents after he was about 10 years old, and I just chalked up a lot of his early behavior to anger he had towards them."

Duane watches her eyes as she speaks, shaking his head in disbelief.

"I realized later, in therapy, that he had never told me he loved me or ever even said the word love about anyone or anything. He only said he wanted me, wanted things, almost in the exact same way. When he didn't think he was treated right, he wanted to destroy people, things. He had also been violent at work. But while it was happening, my B in Psychology 101 hadn't prepared me for someone with his severity of mental problems. I was so, so naive."

She takes a deep breath and continues on, not seeing Duane's pained expression and sad eyes as he listens to her saga.

"I found out later he beat up a kid at his high school so badly that the boy almost died. The fight was over a cell phone the boy said Al was trying to steal from him. He got expelled from high school and spent time in a juvenile detention facility for two years after that incident. That all came out in court." Laura's eyes start to tear up.

"And, then, of course, the lies about his background and then his inability to keep any job he got. For a while, he'd leave in the morning, telling me he was heading for work and then I found out he'd been fired weeks before and was just driving around town. Occasionally, he'd pick up day work on construction sites."

Duane returns to the kitchen table for the wine bottle, pours himself another glass.

"Did he actually believe he could just kill you and immediately collect everything your parents left you in their will?"

"Since he never testified in court, I guess I'll never know for sure, but basically, yes. Despite me wanting to believe that he was a college graduate with a business degree from the University of Texas, he was, in reality, a high-school drop-out with a criminal record. Talk about a distorted picture!"

Duane shakes his head again, "And you were a newspaper reporter and someone who should be very skeptical and you didn't see any holes in his stories?"

"My brother told me later that he didn't think his stories about his background added up but our parents had just died and he saw that Al was making me happy. Ed said that, for the first time, he thought I was in love. He didn't want to ruin it and hoped, really hoped, his analysis about Al was wrong. Ed later said that he, too, was pretty naive. Remember, Al's a con-man, though, and pretty good at it."

Duane shakes his head and takes a long drink of wine.

"My first real clues, looking back, were early, just two months into our marriage. Once he came home with his hands and knuckles bloody, like he'd been in a fight, but he told me his injuries happened when he changed a tire on the car. I didn't check for several days, but the spare tire he said fell on his hands was dusty and had not be removed from the trunk of the car. When I confronted him, he flew into a rage."

"Did you ever tell anyone?"

She shakes her head, looking down at the floor. "No. I felt that would be admitting failure and bad judgment. I just couldn't believe how different he had become from what he was like before we were married. I started to realize I was living a nightmare."

"Would you call him sociopathic?" Duane says in an official tone as if he were investigating a crime.

"I don't know if he was clinically sociopathic, but I discovered that he was a violent con-man who was unable to hold a job, and he had more than a dozen different ones in that two-year period. He was an oil-rig manager when we got married. That lasted two months. Then car salesman, construction foreman, plumber and like that. Each time he lost the job by getting into fights, I learned later, at the trial."

"So, you paid all the household bills?" Duane asks.

"Yes and his truck payments. All that time, he continued to be more jealous of my career and the money I brought in."

Duane looks puzzled, then frowns, "I don't get it. Did all his anger come from being abandoned by his parents and being raised in foster homes? Did he ever even go to a training school? How could he fake knowing how to work on an oil rig or do plumbing? What's the deal with his obsession with money and things?"

Laura listens, shakes her head and shrugs her shoulders. "My therapist told me not to even try to look for any logic in Al's behavior. It's something normal people always try to do. Dr. Marshall said simply that crazy people are crazy. Period. Sane people can't figure them out and victims of that craziness, like me, ultimately, if they ever want to live normal lives, have to try to forgive the person, then forget them, and just let it go."

"Yeah, right," Duane says cynically. "That may be good advice, but have you forgiven him, forgotten him?"

Laura looks at the floor. "If I had either forgiven or forgotten him, would I be living way up in a remote area and going above timberline every chance I get?" she asks back in a sarcastic tone. "Maybe I'd be able to get into a regular bed and pull the sheets up over me. Ride in my car with the top down. Ya think?"

"Sorry. I believe you're actually doing good, under the circumstances," he says, looking sad. "Still, what did he have that blindsided you?"

"Well, Al, as you could see, was extremely good looking and persuasive. He could convince the devil to go to confession, as they say." Laura states.

"To me, he does seem to be a classic sociopath, no conscience at all," Duane says, sounding like a cop writing a report. "They're often very good looking, know how to twist people around their fingers. As you say, con men! Big time con men. Often dangerous and violent."

"You've got the picture. Guess he thought he'd just marry me, kill me and collect. Wham, bam, thank you, ma'am. Took him about 18 months to figure out how. The psychiatrist who testified at the trial said he was more of a psychopath. Pure and simple."

"I've seen lots of police reports and read research when I went to the police academy in Los Angeles. But this? This is cold. Bizarre! You're so lucky to be here! Left for dead in a tool box? Thank God for that grave digger!"

"Yep. He literally saved me. And an old lady who lived near the cemetery refused to give up on me, too. I'll tell you about her one day."

"Pretty damned weird, I'd say. Even as a cop, I never heard anything quite like it."

"Told ya."

"Did they ever locate the guy you heard helping Al lift the tool box into the mausoleum?"

"No. Police thought he was maybe a day worker from across the Mexico border that Al hired on a street corner. Guy probably didn't know which end was up. Even the fingerprints they found were identified only as Al's, the grave digger's and those of the police officers who rescued me."

Sounding like a detective, Duane adds, "Probably wore gloves."

Laura starts to tear up, wipes her eyes with her hands and looks again into the fire.

Duane reaches over and takes her hand, "I've got some advice for ya. Steer clear of those scumbag hippies and their wolves. You need to be around normal people for a while." Duane smiles, pauses, and adds, "Like me."

He puts his arm around her and pulls her close. She doesn't pull away.

28

Fireworks and Moonlight

At Timberline Ranch, preparations are underway for the Fourth of July. Bunting is being draped over the ranch's dining room doorway and hung from the upstairs balconies. Red, white and blue balloons are nearby, ready to be inflated. The hay rack sports a new sign, "Fireworks Thursday Night."

Laura prepares to lead another group on a trail ride. Jerry helps them onto their horses. This group of 10 includes two older couples and another man in his 30s who looks nervous and uncomfortable. Laura eyes him with curiosity. She feels she has seen him before but can't place him.

"Thanks again, Laura. Now I can help Vince get things ready for the fireworks show comin' up this week. Takes more time than you'd think. You're really helping us out."

"I actually like playing trail guide. First job I've had that didn't require writing. Also the first one that lets me ride a horse!" she smiles.

"Your pay kinda sucks, though," Jerry laughs.

"Yeah, probably less than 25 cents an hour, if that. Keeps me from going bonkers in my cabin, though. That's worth something!"

"Right," Jerry says, tightening the cinch around the last horse.

"By the way, what's with that guy?" Laura whispers gesturing behind her with her head toward the man standing apart from all the others.

"Been here a while now. Name's Brian. Asked me about them hippies. I think he's an author or somethin', maybe writing a book."

"Really?"

"Yep, told me he used to work with 'em a few years ago in Alaska. He's kind of an odd duck."

Laura turns around to look over at Brian. He notices her staring and looks away.

"Probably just another weirdo," Laura says under her breath as she gets on Solo and starts lining up the dudes.

The day is perfect. Temperature is about 75, clear blue sky with no wind. Rain clouds are missing entirely.

"This is the kind of weather tourists come to Montana for," Laura announces to the smiling group. "Enjoy your Chamber of Commerce poster day. No extra charge."

The dudes grin back. Riding their horses, smiling, chatting and taking occasional photos becomes something Laura views as a collage of dude-ranch guests. They all seem to have a good time, enjoying the trail rides and never complaining much about anything but the weather. In many ways it's a perfect job for this time in her recovery. No demands, no stress and no worries.

Once they reach the beaver pond, Laura is in her element. Food is distributed, horses are tied and the people all have settled down to eat, take pictures or just lie on the grass and enjoy the view.

Brian remains alone until the others are occupied elsewhere and then comes up to where Laura and Destiny are relaxing. He says nothing as she gives Destiny a milk bone and takes a sandwich out of the brown bag. Brian awkwardly holds his lunch bag but seems more distracted as if he wants to ask her something but can't get the words out.

Just then, a group of big-horn sheep are spotted standing above timberline on a rocky outcropping overlooking the pond. One man points them out to the others and everyone in the group begins to take photos using cell phones, digital cameras, video cameras.

Brian does not. He squats down next to Laura and nervously fidgets, pulling up grass and throwing it aimlessly as he begins to talk.

"I heard from Jerry at the ranch that you sorta know the Ballards up at Los Lobos Cabin?" he asks rather than states.

Laura smiles at his words and chuckles, "We haven't exactly met formally. I didn't even know their last name."

"I taught school with them in Alaska. Evie and I were actually engaged before she met Gregg. She was still Evie Bernier then."

"Gregg came up to Akiak after she and I had taught there a year. That kinda changed my life."

Brian stops talking, picks up a small stone and throws it. It makes a splash in the pond. Destiny jumps and looks as if she thinks it's a piece of wood to retrieve. One man sees her reaction and throws a stick into the pond. She plops in, swims and brings it back to him.

Laura waits for Brian to continue talking but he is silent, obviously in his own thoughts. She tries to continue the conversation.

"People up here wonder how they make a living from way up there among the rocks and so far from anything or anybody," she says, not looking at Brian.

"Easy to figure out. Gregg's written a couple of books on the Yupik people, the Eskimos, you know? They're used in universities all over the world. Google his name and find out."

Laura puts on her journalist's hat and remains quiet, not staring at Brian but hoping he'll continue to talk.

"Lives off royalties, investments too, probably," he adds.

Brian stops talking again for a few seconds and Laura interjects, "He looks a lot older than her."

"Yep, and I just couldn't compete with his worldly experience, his books, his money. Evie was kinda swept off her feet by him."

Laura stands and heads over to where the horses are tied. Brian follows. They continue their conversation. Destiny gets excited and runs over to them.

"Gregg's at least 20 years older than Evie. More like a father than a husband, the father she was looking for and didn't have."

Laura takes mental notes.

Brian's tone changes to confidential, "She'd been abused by her real dad. Has a hard time trusting anyone. Anyone but her animals that is."

Laura stares and then blinks as if she has just realized something about herself. Her tone is somber. "Yeah, nature's one thing. Human nature's quite another."

She pats Solo and starts to repack the saddle bags with empty water bottles, lunch leftovers and trash.

Brian helps.

When they finish, he reaches into his back pocket and takes out a dog-eared photo from his wallet to show Laura.

"That's us, me and Evie," he says, handing the photo to her.

Laura looks at Evie and Brian dressed in parkas and mukluks in front of a snowmobile, smiling. Deep snow surrounds them.

"After she fell in love with Gregg, we all three still kinda remained friends. More or less." His facial expression conflicts with his words.

He places the photo back into his wallet and stares blankly.

"Besides, I'm really a city guy and I knew she'd never be happy with me. Gregg had the money to buy her the space she needed. He did everything to win her over. In fact, he spoiled her rotten."

The dudes, ready for the ride back to the ranch, have remounted their horses and have begun to follow Laura's lead as the sun starts to slip behind the highest mountains. Spectacular colors paint an awe-inspiring scene. No one speaks for a while. As he rides his horse parallel to Laura's and talks in a confidential tone, Brian almost whispers, "Mind going back up with me tomorrow to see them? I wrote them that I'd come this week."

Laura looks at him with surprise.

He adds, "I even rented a four-by-four so I could drive up there, but I'd kinda like to ride the horses again. If you'd come, too."

Laura looks at him, considering the offer. She's too curious, too much the journalist to turn him down. Although everything logical screams at her to decline, she hears herself agreeing, "Sure. I'd actually like to officially meet them. I've gotten some pretty strange impressions."

The group continues riding quietly until the ranch comes back into view.

29

Timberline Bound

It's cloudy. Brian and Laura ride their horses to the top of the hill overlooking Los Lobos Cabin. Destiny is not with them. They stop at the overlook. Laura seems apprehensive. They survey the cabin and wolf compound. Brian seems surprised to spot the wolves, who appear to be in a state of unrest, pacing, yipping, growling.

They both simultaneously spot Evie as she comes out on the cabin's porch and looks up the hill toward them waving her hands excitedly.

From the distance, she appears to be a flower child gone to seed. She sees them on the hill waving, and she waves back. Brian smiles and seems upbeat for the first time.

Feeling a bit of an interloper, Laura asks, "You sure you still want me along?"

"Positive," he says without hesitation, "You'll see. They're neat people. Bit eccentric, maybe, but neat."

"Don't mention her black eye," Laura says.

Brian looks puzzled, "Huh?"

"You heard me!" Laura says emphatically.

They ride down the hill. Gregg comes down the stairs to greet them and helps tie the horses to part of the chain-link fence. But he doesn't seem to recognize Laura as someone he has seen recently.

Evie wears a thin and dirty flowered skirt and a stained purple tee shirt. Her hair is lifeless, pulled back with a piece of rag. She looks more eccentric, much older than in Brian's photo. She has put on makeup to cover the purple around her eye. The eye is still somewhat swollen but she has obviously tried to mask it.

Evie stares at Brian. She gives him a long hug and an almost sensuous kiss on the lips. Brian responds but seems uncomfortable at the length of the embrace. He gently disengages himself. He looks at her almost as if he's never seen her before. He shakes hands with Gregg.

Laura's own observation techniques mastered over several years of watching people's reactions in courts, in interviews and during protests, are in full function. She finds group dynamics fascinating and often gets lost in analyzing them. She watches Gregg who continues to stare at Evie and Brian with disdain.

As they pass the fenced-in compound, the wolves seem excited, standing up against the chain-link fence, whining a welcome, their ears back. They prance around, spiraling and yipping.

Evie speaks slowly, mysteriously, and confidentially to Brian.

"The wolves told me you were coming; they know my heart."

Brian looks chagrined, as if he's sorry he came, sorry he dug up the past. He smiles a crooked smile.

"They could feel you approaching," Evie adds.

Brian looks even more uncomfortable. He avoids her eyes.

"Brian, you just look wonderful!" Evie exclaims.

"Ah, er you do too. Both of you. Must be the mountain air!"

Gregg smirks at Brian's disingenuous comment.

Brian awkwardly gestures toward Laura. "Oh, this is Laura Black. Gregg and Evie Ballard. She says her dog annoyed you a while back."

Evie frowns and looks puzzled and then shakes her hand as if Brian has gotten something mixed up.

Gregg's tone is not as forgiving as his words. He gruffly says, "No harm done. Her pooch just set off the wolves one day."

He doesn't elaborate, mention the gunshots or shake her hand.

"Sorry 'bout that," Laura says. "Nice to finally meet you both."

Neither Evie nor Gregg comment.

They all walk toward the cabin and stop at the wolf compound's gate in front of the largest male wolf. Evie calls him by name and

Kusko seems to instantly recognize Brian. The wolf lifts his paw and "smiles" back.

Brian immediately unlocks the chain-link gate and enters the enclosure. As he walks in, Laura holds her breath. Instantly, she senses that Brian is in grave danger, but within seconds she changes her mind and is stunned at what takes place.

Kusko stands, places his paws on Brian's shoulders and tries to lick his face. Brian speaks to the wolf in Yupik, then English.

Laura is startled to hear what she believes is the Eskimo language flow out so easily from Brian and is in disbelief while watching a full-sized wolf interact with a human being, someone from years past.

"Kusko! You ol' thing you!"

The Alpha male continues to show his teeth, clicking them almost as if talking. He has direct eye contact with Brian and dances around, his ears flat against his head.

Brian squats down to eye level with the wolf, totally at ease with him. Evie and Gregg do not appear surprised. Laura cannot take her eyes off the wolf and Brian as they seem to communicate.

Suddenly, a large female trots toward Brian and comes between Kusko and him. Brian also speaks to her in Yupik, then calls her Tundra in English. Kusko snaps at Tundra jealously.

Evie smiles with delight as Brian announces, "And is this my Tundra? You're such a big lady now, and a Mommy too?"

Gregg adds with a smirk, "And making Kusko jealous as hell, just like a woman!"

The symbolism isn't lost on Laura who has seen Gregg glaring at Evie since she gave Brian the sloppy kiss.

"Nothing's changed. Always were jealous of each other since the beginning," Brian says looking at Gregg.

Laura's eyes widen as she seems to understand that neither man is speaking of wolves.

Tundra and Kusko continue to vie for Brian's attention. He's torn as to which wolf to pet, which to ignore. Then, he extricates himself, walks back through the gate, pulls it shut but fails to lock it. He joins the others and begins brushing the wolf hair and dirt from his shirt and jeans.

Brian's nonchalance seems to puzzle Laura who continues to look incredulous as the four start toward the cabin.

"They've never forgotten you, Brian. Neither have I, er, we," Evie says staring at Brian. "Let's go inside."

Gregg continues to sulk as he glances at Brian's clothes, haircut and clean-shaven appearance. He looks down at his own dirty gray undershirt. He passes his hand through his unkempt hair and then fingers his matted beard, realizing, as usual, it has the remnants of breakfast in it.

He sucks in his gut as they head inside and makes another swipe at smoothing his hair.

Brian and Evie are arm in arm. Laura walks behind, odd man out.

Next to the front door, they pass a trash can loaded with empty beer bottles and pieces of animal feces. Flies buzz around it.

30

Home Sweet Home

Upon entering the cabin, Laura immediately concludes that if she were assigned to describe the place for a newspaper feature article, the first details she would write would be an overview. She would say it resembles a hunter's shack. Masculine. Stark.

Next she would describe in detail, the large, now-empty power cable spool serving as the table in the small kitchen-family room, eliminating space for any other furniture.

As she returns to reality, Laura spots two badly bent, mismatched metal folding chairs pulled up next to the spool table. In one corner, an old wood-burning stove sits on the badly stained unfinished plywood floor. A splintery wooden bench is pushed up against a grease-stained wall.

A closer looks reveals animal scratch marks on everything—doors, walls, flooring, cabinets, even the spool table's top. She tries to imagine full-grown wolves walking or lying on it while Gregg and Evie eat meals.

An overpoweringly strong urine odor permeates the dwelling, despite all of its open windows bringing in mountain air.

"Please have a seat," Evie says, overly politely gesturing to Laura, as she brushes off a small stool with frayed fabric covering it, causing noticeable amounts of hair and fur to fly from it and land on the floor. Brian sees the falling debris. Laura observes him grimace, but he quickly catches himself, his blank expression instantly returning.

The men take the folding chairs. Evie checks the bench's cleanliness before she sits, wiping some crumbs and more animal hair onto the floor. Gregg notices the filth and sighs, shakes his head.

"We don't get much company," he says, looking slightly embarrassed. "With the wolves coming in here, we don't want to own anything they could ruin."

Gregg gestures toward an adjoining room which can be partially seen. Mattresses cover the entire floor. Dirty and torn fitted sheets cover each one. Some of the stuffing from the mattresses spills out of large tears.

"You might say we've domesticated them. Somewhat. They, er, sleep with us, eat with us. But, unfortunately, they can't be housebroken."

He points at some floor stains and clumps of feces.

Laura tries not to look.

"I've made some fresh bread for us. Want some tea with it?"

Brian, sounding too much like he's trying to please Evie, immediately answers, "Sure. Sounds good. You always were a great cook, if I remember correctly."

Evie smiles and stands, going to a metal bread box which is dented and stained and has heavy clamps to keep its lid on securely. Immediately, Laura pictures wolves trying to break into it.

She, too, feigns enthusiasm but looks wary, wondering how she will be able to eat or drink anything with the stench and the filth ever present, "Oh, yes, fine. Thank you, Evie."

An uncomfortable silence prevails and Laura nervously fills the gap, "So you raised these wolves from pups?"

Evie places tea bags into four badly chipped, stained ceramic mugs and takes a dented kettle which has started to whistle from the small wood-burning stove.

"Yes. Want to see some Alaska videos?" she asks, looking at Brian who says nothing in reply.

Laura nods. Gregg stands and goes to an old VCR sitting atop a television set. He angles the set so they can all see it from the kitchen.

"Great. I'd like to see 'em too," Brian says softly with a far-away look in his eyes. "A lot has happened since those days."

With Gregg occupied, Brian watches Evie, dumbfounded. His eyes look sad as he sees her clothes, her hair, her surroundings.

Gregg turns on the television set and inserts a cassette into the VCR. Everyone's attention shifts to the screen. On the video is an Alaskan village scene with Brian, Evie and Gregg dressed in heavy winter jackets, knit hats and gloves, standing in front of a small school with several Eskimo children and some sled dogs. Evie is seen tossing a large snowball at the camera.

While they watch the screen, Evie brings cups of tea and some pieces of sliced bread on a dented pie tin. "Need sugar for your tea?" she asks.

Laura and Brian shake their heads. Gregg begins to slurp the hot tea. No one touches the bread.

Brian glares at the set. He seems emotional, almost tearful. He bites his lower lip as he watches. The video shows Evie seemingly normal, happy and in love. She hugs Brian and he kisses her cheek. Laura surmises Gregg apparently was shooting the video at this point.

Snow and blue sky surround them. Young and vibrant, Evie takes a handful of snow, kisses her fingers, then blows a snow kiss to Brian, its flakes sparkling toward him in the sunlight.

Seeing the gesture on the screen, Gregg makes a grunting sound and looks away from the set. Laura notices; Brian ignores him or doesn't hear him.

"This really brings back memories," Brian says softly, blinking back to reality as he addresses Laura. "That's where we all spent three years together. That's our school. Our students. Gregg's. Evie's. Mine."

He pauses and becomes too choked up to continue speaking.

Laura smiles and watches as the camera focuses on young Yupik children playing with their sled dogs in the school yard. A younger and more handsome Gregg picks up one young girl and swings her around by her arms. She squeals with delight, saying something in Yupik, which Laura mentally notes resembles German.

Then, Evie's voice interrupts the three viewers and they look toward her, "Let me know when the pups come on. I love that part."

She has rounded up some badly wrinkled paper napkins and begins to distribute them to each person.

"It's just about time for the pups!" Gregg calls to Evie.

She leaves the kitchen and rushes directly to the television set. She sits cross-legged on the dirty, splintery floor, just six or seven inches from it, staring intently at the screen.

"Move to the right, Evie, you're blocking our view!" Gregg grumbles.

Evie complies, moving even farther than she needs to. On screen are four very young and fluffy wolf pups playing in the snow with Brian and Evie who talk to them in Yupik.

"What are you two saying?" Laura asks, looking at Evie, then at Brian for an answer. Both seem enamored with what they are seeing, being transported back to a special time and place. Both smile, then look at one another, then back at the screen.

Gregg finally ends the silence. "They're speaking Yupik, the language everyone, all the natives, speak up there."

"Our original wolves still only understand Yupik. Their offspring understand English," Evie adds.

Then, suddenly, Evie gets on all fours and crawls even closer toward the screen. She mumbles in Yupik and kisses the screen where the wolves appear. Brian and Laura shudder at her bizarre behavior. Gregg sees their reactions and for the first time sounds angry, mean.

"Evie! God damn it! Get the hell up from the fucking floor and get us some more tea, will ya? Fer Christ's sakes!"

Evie stands up, not looking embarrassed at all. She is still smiling and staring at the screen. She walks to the kitchen and returns with the tea kettle.

For the first time Laura notices Evie's hands are dark and crusty with dirt, her fingernails overgrown and caked with black as if she's just been digging in soil.

As Evie reaches over Laura to pour more water into her cup, Laura inhales and blinks her eyes as if smelling something putrid— body odor times a hundred.

Brian notices too and gasps.

Laura holds onto the mug, not sipping or moving, trying not to grimace. She casually wipes its rim. Evie again offers each of them a piece of bread. It looks anything but appetizing.

Laura reluctantly takes a piece as does Brian. They sit awkwardly, trying to balance their mugs of tea and pieces of bread. Evie doesn't notice; her eyes return to the screen again as she noisily gobbles, slurps.

The video begins to show a progression of short scenes taken at various times of the year in several locations as the wolves get older. One, taken when the river was frozen solid, shows the wolf pups being carried out onto the ice on a snowmobile. Gregg places them on the ice and they begin to slip and slide, almost like they're swimming on it while Gregg, Brian and Evie laugh hysterically.

The three of them, now seeing the scene again, burst out laughing. Brian and Gregg do a quick high five.

Suddenly, outside the cabin, the wolves begin to yap and scratch at the cabin's front door. Laura seems to be the only one who has heard them over the laughter.

"What's that?" she asks loudly.

Evie stands to open the door and makes a shrill yelping sound. "Eeeeeooooooeeek!" She throws open the door.

"How'd you all get out? Thought Brian locked the gate."

Eight wolves, sans Tundra and her pups, noisily bound inside. Laura immediately sits frozen in place.

31

Jail Break

Meanwhile, back at the ranch, Jerry rakes straw around to clean the corral. Destiny sits unleashed nearby.

Both Jerry and Destiny stop as a shrill animal cry echoes through the canyon. At first it sounds like a coyote, then maybe a wolf. Jerry stops working, scratches his head and then resumes raking. Destiny sits transfixed, her head cocked, ears forward.

As a group of guests begins to ride out of the corral on horseback, Destiny, as if she's been summoned, races to follow.

Startled and upset, Jerry screams, "Destiny! Come back here! Damn it!"

Destiny dashes away and heads for the loop trail, ahead of the riders. She quickly disappears from view.

Jerry shakes his head in disgust.

32

Welcome to Our Pack

Once the wolves are inside the cabin, Gregg and Evie rush to greet them, welcoming each wolf with a great deal of fanfare, speaking Yupik to some of the wolves, English to others. One large male stands on his hind legs, placing his paws on Evie's shoulders, ears flat and his tail wagging wildly. The wolf licks her lips. She kisses back. Seeing this, Brian wrinkles his nose in dismay as Evie's lips touch the wolf's.

Brian's jaw slightly drops in shock. Gregg instantly stares over to check Brian and Laura's reactions. She looks uncomfortable too.

The wolves who have not already greeted Brian outside slowly approach Laura and him, showing their teeth as if greeting them, tails wagging. They turn, ripple, spiral. Still seated, neither Brian nor Laura puts their hands out to touch them.

Laura sits perfectly still, curious, but following Brian's example, keeps her hands in her lap. She smiles and watches the wolves intently. Their gazes are hypnotic. As a journalist, she is fascinated with their behavior, so different from that of dogs, yet so similar in ways, too.

Brian greets Kusko who again acts as if he is renewing his acquaintance. Kusko, standing almost at the same height as Brian, tries to lick his face. He turns to avoid the wolf's lips. Other wolves hang back out of respect for the Alpha.

Wolves crowd the kitchen, wagging their tails, prancing around.

During the commotion, Brian's main focus returns to the television set which is still showing Alaska with Evie looking young, vibrant and happy. She laughs and rolls in the snow with the wolves in numerous scenes. While everyone's attention is diverted elsewhere, Laura stuffs her piece of bread into her jeans pocket.

Though still petting each wolf as it enters the cabin, Evie's eyes focus on the Alaska video in the background.

The arriving wolves as one unit suddenly seem to have finished interacting with humans and trot to the adjoining room to stretch out on their mattresses.

In the main room, Laura sees a dusty plaque nailed to the wall. It's engraved with a quote. She stands and walks over to it and reads:

The strength of the pack is in the wolf and the strength of the wolf is in the pack.—Rudyard Kipling **The Jungle Book 1894.**

Then, out of nervousness and journalistic habit, she sits back down and begins to interview Evie and Gregg as if she's on assignment.

"So, tell me, what have you two learned from living with wolves?"

Gregg does not seem to hear her question nor is he interested in listening to Evie's answer. He heads toward the refrigerator.

Evie pauses and looks upward, her eyes filling with tears. She doesn't immediately respond to Laura's question. She takes in several deep breaths. Brian suddenly stares at her as if he's looking back in time.

Beer in hand, Gregg, ignoring everyone, looks bored and frowns as if he has heard it all before, even prior to Evie uttering the first word. He sets down the beer, pulls his bag from his shirt pocket, extracts a joint and lights up. He seems to wash down the smoke with swigs of beer.

Laura, remembering what the woman doctor said about the effects of marijuana and alcohol at high altitudes, wonders how long it will be before their super-effects are obvious.

33

Mirrors of the Past

It's mid-afternoon. The patrol car is the only vehicle in the sheriff's sub-station parking lot. Duane sits at his desk and stares blankly out of the window. Then as if an idea suddenly hits him, he turns to open a neatly organized file drawer, taking out a large file folder marked Domestic Violence. He lays it on top of his otherwise perfectly clean desk.

He walks to a small table where he prepares himself a cup of instant coffee and sets the microwave for 45 seconds. When it's ready, he adds a teaspoon of sugar, stirs the coffee and then with a small napkin, wipes off the spoon and replaces it back next to the coffee jar. He sits down, picks up the folder and opens it.

Since Laura has told him about being left for dead by her husband and only being saved by a grave digger and an elderly woman who refused to give up, his perspective has begun to change. Feeling uneasy for possibly not taking domestic-violence complaints more seriously, he has decided to review every case in the county to see if he has underestimated the hidden seriousness of any matters he has handled.

From the top drawer of his desk, he retrieves a yellow legal pad and a pen to take notes as he reads each case.

After two hours, he finds no situations or reports in which it appears he acted sloppily or inappropriately. He's convinced he's been professional and thorough, each time, every time. Then, as he is wiping his coffee cup with a napkin and hanging it back on a hook near the microwave, an uncomfortable feeling sweeps over him. He returns to his desk, picks up his pen and, on the yellow pad he writes one word in all caps, EVIE, retracing the letters again and again until her name jumps off the page.

He circles it and places a large question mark after it. He thinks about her for a moment, pictures her swollen eye and the angry exchanges between the couple described by Laura, and he feels uncertain about how to proceed. He questions if Evie, like Laura, has ever disclosed her troubled home life to anyone.

He ponders a question in his mind, "Who could she even tell, anyway, the wolves?"

His cell phone rings. He checks the number. "Armstrong," he says into the phone, puts down the legal pad and pen, picks up his hat and gun and leaves the building. "I'm on my way."

34

Lessons Learned

At Los Lobos Cabin, another video plays in the background, this one showing wolves play-fighting, and sharing an animal carcass that Gregg drags to them over the snow. It has been a few minutes between when Laura asked the question and when either Gregg or Evie seem motivated to answer her.

Several times on screen the wolves look directly into the camera, their amber eyes fixed in eerie stares. Laura, Brian and Evie say nothing. Gregg, for the first time, appears nostalgic and sad as he watches his life in Alaska from his present home. He looks somber. Brian and Evie continue to stare at the video of a life they have both left behind.

When Evie finally breaks the silence, she measures her words. She looks spiritual, far-away. Her voice is musical, her words poetic. She seems to see no one else in the room and she has stopped watching the video.

"The Yupik people have a saying, it goes, 'To look into the eyes of a wolf is to look into your own soul.'"

Laura, hearing the quote, wishes she were able to write down some notes about Evie's demeanor, her tone of voice, the contrast between her life in Alaska and today, including this quote of quotes. She knows she'll never forget the interactions and observations, but her journalism training cries out for her to more accurately and more formally document them.

With her comment, Evie has captured the attention of both Brian and Laura who stare at her, waiting for her to continue.

Gregg goes to the refrigerator again, grabs another beer, and plops down on a metal chair. He lights a regular cigarette, takes a few deep drags and then pats his shirt pocket to check the security of his cloth bag of future relief.

Evie, face pointed upward, closes her eyes and continues, "From wolves I have learned to look inward."

She pauses, opens her eyes fully, looks only at Brian and continues, "I could never be as courageous as a wolf, or as loyal to my mate or offspring. I could never honor my family as they do, putting my pack before everything."

Brian's eyes glisten but he makes no move to hide his emotions. He stares back as if his mind is on rewind and he is reliving their joyous days gone by.

For several seconds no one speaks.

Laura finally says softly, "I've heard wolves actually mate for life."

Evie opens her eyes and her tone shifts to a more academic one, "Yes, that's true in good times. It's only when they feel in danger or are starving that they will mate with others for the pack's survival."

Laura notices and wonders if Evie is giving Brian some kind of a symbolic signal. If so, Brian's face doesn't reveal that he hears or understands.

Evie stares at Brian again and keeps her eyes on him for an uncomfortably long time. He seems to feel her staring, then glances at her and looks back at the video which is showing a celebration at their school in Alaska. The classroom is crowded with parents and Yupik elders in traditional costumes, the first glimpse of adults in the village that Laura has seen.

Then Brian speaks directly to Evie, "Remember when that Yupik elder once told us that the Alpha male wolf teaches mankind to think of their mates and their children first? I remember him saying that if they thrive, then his pack survives."

Evie smiles and nods knowingly saying, "Yes, even when people talked about getting married, many used the term *wolfing* to mean getting married forever." She points to the Kipling quote on the wall plaque gesturing for Brian to read it.

Brian stands and walks over to it. He remains facing the wall for a few seconds after reading the short quote. He seems to be avoiding more eye contact with Evie.

With music from the school celebration in the background, Laura shrugs and mumbles under her breath to herself, "Wish all mates were that loyal."

As distinct snoring emanates from the roomful of wolves, a contrasting scene appears on the television screen. Young, energetic wolves frolic and play in the snow. They begin to howl as young Evie and Brian howl along with them on the screen.

The sound is eerie, compelling.

A couple of the sleeping wolves in the adjoining room seem to stir, perhaps dreaming, perhaps hearing their own cries on the video. Low tones and guttural sounds from the room blend together for a few seconds and then cease.

Evie looks over at Gregg sitting at the spool table seemingly waiting to answer Laura's question about lessons learned from wolves. He continues staring at Laura and when she finally looks over at him, he begins what sounds like a summary of the entire subject. His comments seem directed only toward her and also sound oddly academic and thoughtful although his speech has become somewhat slow and slurred.

"You didn't ask me directly what wolves have taught me but I can tell you it is very simple: one's behavior can be misjudged by ignorant people."

Laura considers his comment without making her own. He says nothing further.

When Evie speaks, she sounds ethereal. "Yes, wolves have been poisoned and massacred, when, in fact, they were just being wolves."

Laura adds, "I guess old folk tales haven't helped much either. The big bad wolf has gotten some very bad press."

She smiles at her own clever wording. Nobody else does. She seems to be talking to herself. The other three continue to watch the video, alone in their own worlds, going back in time.

Again from the adjoining room, more snoring and deep breathing continue from the sleeping pack. Evie tiptoes over to the room's doorway and gestures for Brian and Laura to come over to her and look in. The two stand next to her as Evie whispers, "Now I ask you, do they look ferocious and evil?"

The wolves, as if one massive animal, snooze, grunt, snuggle. Kusko, sensing their presence, suddenly becomes alert, bolts up and takes the position of guarding his pack, his eyes fixed on the entry to the room. He does not move from his sentry position until Evie enters, lies down on the mattresses and begins to roll around with the wolves, playing. Then, Kusko also relaxes and stretches out with her. The others awaken, yawn and start to play. Evie's skirt comes up and reveals her worn and stained underpants.

Brian, who is watching her, frowns and turns away.

Laura watches his reaction.

He seems to be muttering under his breath at Evie. Laura tries to hear what he's saying, but he's talking too softly, although he's obviously upset.

Gregg joins them and leans in to see Evie on the mattresses with the writhing wolves. He shakes his head in disgust, says nothing. He heads for the refrigerator to get another beer. He empties half of it on the first pull and says, "It's always an emotional battle, whether to keep them wild or tame them."

Laura wonders to herself if Gregg is referring to wolves or wives.

Evie whispers again, as if talking to the wolves, not Gregg, "Captive or free? A question we may never fully answer."

Just then, Laura is shocked to hear Destiny barking on the cabin's porch, peering through the open kitchen window and wagging her tail.

Laura's tone is one of frustration and concern. "What the? Oh, great!"

Evie dashes onto the porch before Laura can move. She takes Destiny's head in her hands and speaks soothingly to her, kissing her nose.

"My goodness me, look who's come calling!" Evie coos to Destiny.

Destiny immediately settles down as Evie strokes her and looks into her eyes. By the time Laura arrives at Destiny's side, the dog is clearly captivated by Evie's tone and affection.

Laura looks impressed and freaked out all at once. Destiny has never been that easy to control without constant treats.

"So sorry, Evie. Don't know how Destiny got up here!" she says. "Jerry down at Timberline was supposed to keep her tied up."

Evie addresses Destiny again speaking directly to her and looking into her eyes, "You're too sweet for words; too sweet to be tied up anywhere for any reason, aren't you girl?"

Destiny appears mesmerized.

The words "dog whisperer" suddenly flash through Laura's mind.

Evie waits for a few seconds with her head tilted as if hearing something. She seems to be listening to the dog and she turns to talk directly to Laura, "She was worried about you. Didn't know where you went."

Laura shudders at Evie's remark.

Brian doesn't appear to have heard anything either woman has said.

Destiny continues to lick Evie's face and hands and stare into her eyes. Then as Laura grabs Destiny's collar, Evie goes back inside the cabin, returning with a Ziploc bag. She quickly and almost secretly hands the bag to Laura, holding it carefully to avoid crushing its contents and says, "To heal yourself, learn from nature. You'll become wise and you'll see that nature can give you strength."

Seeing Laura's backpack on the kitchen floor, Evie picks it up and signals for her to put the plastic bag inside it, holding her finger to her mouth to indicate, "Our secret."

Laura complies, carefully placing the bag in an outer pocket and returns with Evie to where Destiny waits quietly on the porch.

Brian and Gregg amble outside seemingly unaware of any unusual interactions between Laura, Evie and Destiny. But, after just a few seconds, Brian looks increasingly uncomfortable. His eyes become steely and he stares at Evie, then looks down at her sandals. His face changes as if he's repulsed by her bare feet, crusty with dirt, and her long and yellowed toenails. His eyes narrow. He looks as if he smells something foul.

He blurts out, "Laura, we really gotta get the horses back," looking away from Evie and adding almost forcefully, "Need to get Destiny back, too."

Laura reads his discomfort and nods, "Yeah, before she sets all the wolves off like she did before."

Looking relieved that Brian is leaving, Gregg goes inside the cabin, quickly shuts the windows to secure the sleeping wolves and pulls the door to the porch closed as he returns.

The foursome plus Destiny begin to walk slowly down the stairs from the cabin, strolling past a special section of the compound where Tundra and her pups play. The pups mob Tundra, biting her ears and tail. She lies down and patiently endures her offspring who roughly begin nursing and pushing one another to settle on a preferred location.

Tundra seems to be acknowledging the smiling onlookers. Kusko has somehow jumped from one of the windows Gregg missed closing and he races from the cabin into the compound gate to be as close to Tundra as possible, guarding her from intruders.

Immediately, he lies down and places his left front paw and leg over her body, careful to not disturb the nursing pups. He seems to be protecting her.

Evie points to Kusko's behavior and says to Laura, "See that? He's hugging his mate and expressing that he's there for her. Tell me they're not affectionate!"

Brian begins walking more rapidly toward the horses without comment. Gregg, Evie and Laura follow him. Some of the wolves have also exited from the cabin's open window and have run back through the open gate to their compound where they begin to eat and drink from large dirty bowls placed on the ground. They notice Evie and Gregg walking away from them and begin to whine for attention.

Destiny momentarily has lagged behind, watching the wolves, this time wagging her tail. They don't seem threatened by her presence nor are they interested in her. She trots to where the horses and the foursome are standing.

When Laura unties his reins and mounts Solo, Evie suddenly realizes Brian is actually departing and immediately she begins to gush at him.

"Thanks so much for coming, Brian. We didn't even get to talk about what you've been doing. Can you please come back up again before you leave?"

Gregg glares at her. Unseen by anyone but Laura, his pursed lips restate the words, his head moving from side to side in cynical mocking, "Can you please come back?"

"No, sorry, Evie. Actually I fly out tomorrow night from Bozeman. Gonna miss the fireworks day after tomorrow, too. It's been great seeing you, though. I'll write you, er, both."

Gregg, looking bored, seems to want the socializing to end immediately. His tone is cool, "Well, okay then, we'll say goodbye for now. And, um, thanks for stopping by."

He grabs Evie's shoulder and roughly pulls her toward him. As her injured eye area touches his upper arm, she winces.

Laura speaks in a rote manner, "Nice meeting you both."

Gregg shakes hands dutifully with Brian who has extended his. Then, Evie extricates herself from Gregg, goes to Brian and hugs him for an uncomfortably long time. Her eyes begin to glisten.

Gregg scowls.

Laura doesn't know where to look. She turns Solo around and urges him to begin walking. Destiny follows her.

When Brian mounts his horse, the wolves immediately begin to howl as one mournful chorus. It's as though they're reflecting Evie's sadness. When the horses are a quarter mile away, just heading over the rise from Los Lobos Cabin, Brian and Laura hear an unusually eerie whining sound above the chorus. It first sounds like a wolf, then at closer listening, they recognize the high-pitched human voice.

35

Riding in Clouds

Solo expertly leads the way back to the loop trail. Destiny happily follows close behind. Brian and Laura are literally, physically, just along for the ride. Each seems to be in another place, another time, continuing on in silence, neither acknowledging to the other what they've just left behind.

As they approach the beaver pond, in the distance they hear screaming between Evie and Gregg. They suddenly look at one another and grimace as the couple's angry voices eerily echo through the canyon. Still, neither speaks.

After arriving at the pond, Brian's emotions begin to change. Laura stops Solo, allowing him to drink from the pond and graze on bits of tender grass along the water's edge. Brian pulls up next to her and his horse follows suit. They remain on their horses side-by-side, both staring straight ahead across the pond to the rocky outcropping just above timberline.

Destiny, looking tired from her long trip up and back, takes a drink of the pond water, lies down and falls asleep in the grass.

Out of the corner of her eye, Laura sees Brian's jaw tighten and his eyes narrow. Suddenly he begins to describe how he's feeling about Evie now that he has found her again.

"Evie stole four years of my life! Until I saw her again, I just couldn't seem to get over her, feeling all this time I was still in love with her. Everyone I dated always seemed shallow and vacant compared to her."

He doesn't look at Laura for affirmation or reaction. She might as well be elsewhere. As he's getting all of his frustrations off his chest, Laura begins to recognize herself in him, also having ranted to Dr. Marshall about Al.

Brian's words mimic those she used. She shudders, realizing that even his tone parallels what she must have sounded like.

Laura visualizes herself, watching him intently and listening as he verbally explodes. She feels the saddle and Solo under her, but emotionally she can hear herself shouting while leaping to her feet from the therapist's couch to stand facing him.

Brian continues to vent, "I've met women, really nice, good ones, that I should continue relationships with, but they always drop me because I constantly talk about Evie this, Evie that."

Laura nods in commiseration, but she notices Brian ratcheting up, becoming more angry, more frustrated as he talks. His pitch amps up and he appears outraged, almost out of control.

"Nobody wants to hear about your ex-fiancé, your ex-girlfriend, your adventurous teaching job in Alaska, or even the newborn wolf pups the two of us found. Finally, I just stopped dating and took a minimum-wage tutoring job. I became a hermit, no social or even professional interactions."

He takes a quick breath.

"Then I couldn't think of anything but planning this trip to see Evie, saving my pennies and finally coming up here, dreaming about how I could convince her to come back to me. I even planned to ask her in our own Alaska way to marry me. I fantasized about asking her to stay *wolfing* with me forever."

As he utters the last word, he looks repulsed by it.

"Come back to me? Christ! Now, I look at her and despise everything she is and everything she's made me become. I don't have a good job, and I don't have any money and I can't have her the way she used to be."

Tears of anger and frustration begin to roll down his cheeks.

"Thanks to her, I've lost four fucking years!" he screams, looking totally distraught and wiping tears away. "She's lost nothing, nothing at all! I hate her! I hope she gets her just rewards!"

Laura, after hearing his soliloquy, is mute, not only because of the content of his message but because of his delivery. He looks furious, vengeful. He is frightening her. She sees Al in him.

Her days on the newspaper again resurface as she remembers visiting a Texas prison for the insane where she did research for an article about inmate abuse. Many of the prisoners had similar looks on their faces and raged in vengeful tones about family members or prison guards they wanted to see suffer.

Fear sweeps over her as she digests what Brian has just said. She doesn't want to believe it, but she suddenly feels there's a definite question about how he'll proceed in the hours and days ahead.

"Surely he doesn't want to do harm to Evie," she rationalizes in silence, trying to convince herself. "He wouldn't hurt her, would he?"

36

Just the Facts, Ma'am

Duane is in uniform. He and Laura sit at Crystal's in the back booth next to the big picture window. She's talking non-stop. He looks like he wants her to get to the bottom line. He sips his coffee, drums his fingers on the table and finds himself wanting to be anywhere but there with her. Too much information.

"Anyway, Evie, the wolf woman, is totally wacko and I think in love with this Brian guy who I rode up there with, and…" Duane cuts her off.

"I got all that. Tell me about the wolves."

"That was the best or maybe the worst part," she begins relating every gesture, grimace, comment, adding her own psychological analysis. "And, they are really excellent role models for humans because they mate for life, are loyal to their pack, care desperately for their young, sharing all the duties with the pack and they put family first!"

Instead of looking bored, Duane begins to take a few notes, writing them on his yellow legal pad. He writes the words: *mate for life, loyal, family first* and begins to underline them again and again, not appearing to hear anything Laura continues to say.

She describes each video segment, especially ones involving the wolves when Brian and Evie frolic in the snow with the tiny wolf pups.

"The pups seemed totally dependent upon them. Like their kids. After their romp, they put the pups inside their parkas to keep them warm. Their mother was killed by a moose. Kicked in the head. Brian and Evie saw the whole thing near the village where they taught school. They heard her pups crying, found them in the mother wolf's den, almost dead. Brought them home and fed them by bottle.

"That was more than four years ago. Gregg and Evie left when the pups were a year old and moved here. Now, they've interbred and there are about a dozen full-grown wolves and four brand new pups. Darling little fluff balls."

Duane appears less than enthralled with the innumerable details and he suddenly changes the subject. He looks down at his watch.

"They're still wild animals, wolves, for God's sake, Laura," he says forcefully. "Do you think it's possible that Evie could have been attacked by one or more of them?"

Laura suddenly gets a serious look on her face. She stops chattering and takes a breath. "Gads, Duane, I don't know. I don't think they'd do that, but they're so big and powerful-looking with huge teeth. I really don't want to think about what they might do to a human. Creepy!"

She shudders visibly and begins to rub her arms for warmth. She looks into his eyes and says without emotion or sarcasm, "I hate to admit this but I guess that's why you're the cop and I'm not, huh?"

Duane puts his pen down on the legal pad, pushes it sideways near the juke-box unit and reaches across the table to take her hand. He squeezes it lightly. Clearly he wasn't fishing for a compliment and looks surprised at her honesty and sudden change of attitude.

She glances over at the yellow pad and looks puzzled to see and read the only notes he has taken: six heavily underlined words. Of everything she has said for the past half hour, he filtered out and wrote down those few wolf characteristics.

They're the last patrons in the place. Crystal looks like her feet hurt again and stands on one leg, then the other, waiting impatiently at the door with the shade pulled down, the closed sign in place and the keys in her hand. Finally, in frustration, she flips the overhead light switch on and off.

Both Laura and Duane react and immediately stand and walk toward her.

"Gonna have to start charging you two rent," Crystal teases, smiling and patting Laura on the back as she goes out the door.

For the first time, Laura feels as if she is being somewhat accepted. It's the first familiar gesture Crystal has directed toward her.

They descend the stairs together oblivious to Crystal who finally catches Duane's eye as he opens the car door for Laura. Crystal winks and gives him a thumbs up. He ignores her.

Laura and Duane linger as if they don't want to part.

"Well, good night. See you for the fireworks Thursday. I'll meet you there," Laura says, looking as if she would prefer to stay a while.

Smiling, Duane says, "Right. By the way, I notice you chose to completely ignore my advice to stay totally away from those weirdos."

Laura flirts with him with her eyes. "Does that mean you, too?" Duane starts to open his mouth in reply when Laura adds, "Just kidding. Don't worry. I won't be going back up there any time soon."

He waves goodbye and gets into his patrol car. He notices that she's keeping the convertible top up for a few seconds as she starts across the parking lot. Then the top goes down. She waves again, her hand straight up, as they drive off in opposite directions.

37

Fallen Leaves

As she walks through her cabin's front door, Laura remembers the plastic bag still in her backpack and she retrieves it. She touches it gently and remembers Evie's eerie connection to Destiny and her. A pang of guilt sweeps over her for describing Evie to Duane as merely a wacko. After quickly shaking some kibbles into Destiny's dish, and checking on her water-bowl's level, she sits down on the couch and slowly opens Evie's bag.

As she takes out each leaf, she examines it. None is perfect. They have been scarred by wind, rain, heat and the ground itself. Pieces are missing from some, yet overall, they remain intact, their structure still firm.

One particular tiny green leaf stops her. She holds it and remembers a similar sadness she had the year before when vacationing at Watkin's Glen in New York. Dr. Marshall had suggested she go there to view the fall colors. He told her to go alone and commune with nature. She remembered that, like the leaf in Evie's bag, new green leaves were also often torn from their branches along with the mature ones. They all fell at the trunks of trees. Now, touching Evie's collection, she recalls her surprise observation.

Chills sweep over her and she immediately puts down the leaves to flip open and turn on her laptop. In a few clicks and a search through a folder of her writing, she locates an essay she wrote that was later published online in a hiking newsletter.

She reads her own words aloud from the screen. As she does, she feels as if she's never fully understood them until this moment:

Survivor's Spirit

It's early Autumn in New York. The morning air is crisp and the evenings chilly. As I walk through the woods in Watkin's Glen, overlooking the deep and narrow centuries-old gorge where rushing white water continues to carve waterfalls and serpentine rapids from dark shale, I note that most of the trees and shrubs are still green. Foliage clings stubbornly, refusing to yield to the strengthening winds.

But as my eyes scan the forest floor, I see a scattering of fallen leaves of all colors and sizes. First, I examine one tiny green one, still supple and moist, torn from its parent branch. I pick up another leaf, a once-strong part of a mighty oak, wrinkled and bronzed with age but still firm. Others are in graduating colors of yellow, orange, gold and red. All are imperfect, wind-tossed and rain-soaked along life's journey, but none yet surrendering to the inevitable winter ahead.

Sadness sweeps over me as I look up at the still-vibrant leaves fluttering in the cold breeze. I look back down at the now-quiet yet stunningly beautiful specimens on the ground and question Nature. Why them? Why now?

Then a sudden gust creates a whirlwind that lifts some of the fallen ones high above the waters. Some continue to rise out of sight. Others drop onto the tops of waterfalls and begin to tumble downward, only to re-emerge seconds later. Still others stick to the sides of the mossy banks, tucked into calm waters, out of the fray. A few cling to rocky crevices.

These survivors have beaten the odds, defied gravity and shown their unwillingness to lay in wait for winter snow. They dance along the mountain streams toward Lake Seneca and ultimately to the open ocean, symbolically stating, "Not me! Not now! Not now!"

As she finishes reading, Laura looks at the leaves on the coffee table, thinks of Evie's words and realizes their messages were identical.

She sits for several minutes and understands what she wrote was a descriptive story, one that had a personal message but one she didn't fully absorb at the time. It took Evie's pain to make the connection she needed. Evie is a survivor, battered and tossed by life. Laura herself will survive, beat the odds and thrive. Her whirlwind of pain, tragedy and evil will also lift her above the fray to peace. It seems simple, direct and possible now.

After a few more seconds she takes a deep breath, stands, looks at Evie's leaves one last time and gently places them back into the bag to return them to her with deep thanks. She also connects her small printer and makes a copy of her own writing, vowing to give it to Evie as well.

38

Sparkling Night

Patriotic music blares from a tired boom-box. Fireworks fill the sky, lighting up the foothills, reflecting in the ranch lake. The ranch guests watch with delight, but the horses and dogs are not as appreciative, constantly jumping and looking nervous at the sound of each new firecracker or sparkling display. Duane, in uniform, sits with Laura on a log bench.

A group of small children hold sparklers. Laura watches Duane as he looks adoringly at one small boy waving one in wide circles and asks, "Ever want kids?"

Without hesitation, he states, "Definitely! You?"

She smiles back broadly and says, "Same here!"

They sit in silence.

As the program ends with the last, spectacular burst of red, white and blue rockets over the water, the couple strolls hand-in-hand to the parking lot where they get into their separate cars.

After the short drive to Laura's, they enter the front door of her cabin but neither turns on the lights. Moonlight streams in through the opened door.

Destiny tries to get in between them, vying for attention as they stop and hold one another in silence, but she's ignored.

They step inside, close the door. Duane kisses Laura softly, tenderly. She seems overwhelmed and tears stream down her cheeks. She searches his eyes with hers. "I feel so, so torn. I want to, um, to trust you. I, I just."

"This feels right, Laura. For both of us."

Arms entwined, they approach the bedroom.

Destiny tries to follow them, but they shut her out. She lies down in front of the door on a small rug, her head on her paws. Just before dawn, Destiny is still snoring there peacefully and doesn't stir when Duane tiptoes over her and lets himself out the front door.

39

A Person Missing

Just before 10 the following morning, driving into Timberline Ranch, Laura notices Duane's patrol car in the parking lot. She's surprised to see he's at the ranch, knowing it's his routine to be in the sub-station office at mid-morning, doing paperwork from the day before.

Duane is nowhere in sight when Jerry rushes toward her, a concerned look on his face.

Sensing something's wrong, she parks, jumps out of the car, retrieves Destiny's leash from the trunk and attaches it to her collar. "What's up? Where's Duane?" Laura demands rather than asks.

"That hippie woman with the wolves is missing."

"When? How? What are you talking about?" she blurts out, very much a reporter.

"Duane just left for their place in our four-by. Husband come down here to use our phone and reported her missing last night. Her Jeep was found by the side of River Road this morning. Keys inside."

"Wait a minute. Did that Brian guy leave the ranch already?" Laura blurts out.

"Yep. Yesterday afternoon after you two got back from your ride. Went to Bozeman for his flight."

"I need to talk to Duane. I think I can shed some light on this."

Jerry pulls the radio phone out of his back pocket, "Let's see if I can raise him."

"No need. I'll ride on up there. Won't take me long on Solo."

She jogs rapidly toward the barn. Jerry holds Destiny's leash.

"Tie her up, tightly this time!" Laura states firmly. "Really don't need her up there with the wolves; had I known about this I would have left her in my cabin."

40

I Hear Ya, Bro

Laura secures Solo's reins to the chain-link enclosure and walks quickly toward the stairs to Los Lobos Cabin. The ranch 4x4 sits nearby. The Jeep is missing. No wolves are anywhere in sight. The compound's chain-link gate is open. An eerie stillness hangs over the area. As she reaches the cabin's porch, fog rolls in, erasing the 4x4 from her vision field.

It's cold. A chill suddenly runs through her as she visualizes Evie's hands and feet bound by duct tape with another silver strip of it over her mouth. Continuing toward the cabin, Laura forces her mind to return to reality and she tries to imagine Evie and Brian on an airplane, sitting side-by-side holding hands. Try as she will, she cannot get that picture to develop.

The cabin's front door is wide open. She knocks on the door frame and hearing no response, walks inside to see Gregg sitting slumped over at the spool table with his head in his hands. An ashtray near his right elbow overflows with cigarette butts and remnants of joints. He looks drunk and distraught.

Duane, in contrast, is alert and sitting upright, holding his legal pad. He's obviously conducting a professional interview. He's listening to Gregg, watching him and recording facts and impressions. Duane motions for Laura to come in.

Laura closes the door. Every window is open and a foggy breeze rustles scraps of used napkins on the table.

Duane nods a greeting at her. "Jerry just called to say you were coming," he says quietly.

She exchanges a quick but knowing glance with Duane who looks uncomfortable, his large frame dangling over the sides of one of the rickety folding chairs. As she passes him, she squeezes his shoulder lightly and then walks toward the wooden bench.

41

Unwelcome Visitor

Gregg does not look up or acknowledge Laura as she sits down. He continues to talk only to Duane, ignoring her or never actually seeing her arrive at all.

"Can't believe she'd do it! Just can't believe it!" Gregg states to no one in particular.

As Gregg's words hit him, Duane realizes he's not only listening to Gregg but also hearing his own voice once telling his brother, Jim, on the phone about Karen leaving him without warning. The same dumbfounded feeling he experienced back then he now recognizes in Gregg. He stares at him, pities him, understands how drinking was also his own refuge. He can relate to him and knows they share a common contempt for wandering wives.

Gregg continues, "First, she lets the wolves out, then leaves in the middle of the God-damned night!"

"Did you two have an argument?" Duane asks, remembering how many friends asked him that exact question.

Gregg shakes his head, lights up a joint and sucks in the smoke, filling his lungs and blurring his pain.

42

Victim's View

As minutes pass and Gregg seems to be trying to convince Duane that his and Evie's life together was mostly peaceful and quiet, Laura smirks, remembering Evie's black eye and more than once hearing their angry exchanges echo through the canyon.

She glances around the kitchen. Empty beer bottles are everywhere. A nearly empty half-gallon bottle of Jack Daniels sits directly in front of Gregg on the spool table.

He sips an unidentified amber liquid from a glass mug, his face contorting after he downs in one gulp what is left in the hazy container.

"Christ!" he explodes, pounding his fist on the table, startling Laura and Duane and sending more debris onto the floor, "She always said they were like our kids. But she knows they'll die alone out there in the woods. I'm not sure they would even know how to hunt."

His words become more slurred; he starts to sob.

"We raised 'em on super-market chicken, for Christ's sakes! She even cooked roast beef for them sometimes. We spoiled them rotten. They ate better than most people do."

Laura and Duane lock eyes. Duane raises his eyebrows as if to ask, "What do we do now? Any ideas?"

She shrugs back and suddenly takes over interviewing Gregg, "Can you think of any reason she'd leave you or of any place she'd go without transportation?"

Gregg wipes his eyes and nose on his sleeve, then shakes his head.

She asks a follow-up question before he can answer. "Any place she'd want to travel? Anyone who would pick her up?"

Duane begins to look peeved as she has completely usurped his interrogation. She notices him leaning forward, getting his pen and pad ready as if to signal her to butt out. Gregg remains silent, looking as if he knows the answer but doesn't want to reveal it. His lips tighten in a child-like manner.

Both Duane and Laura wait for his response. Duane smirks and shakes his head when Laura butts in again, "You think your friend Brian might know something? Could they have left together?"

Gregg frowns, then looks over accusingly at Laura and narrows his eyes, "Not a chance! You were here. You think she'd leave me for that piss-ant kid? He's never had any money, never will."

Looking surprised at her ability to get Gregg to talk, Duane rapidly scribbles notes.

She continues, "I really don't know. But, Brian did tell me on the ride back to the ranch that he and Evie had been very close over the years, even said they had been engaged at one point."

Duane makes another note and smiles slightly at Laura, which she welcomes.

"Stupid bitch!" Gregg says staring directly and angrily at Laura who glances at Duane, raising her eyebrows to see if he can decipher if Gregg is talking about Evie or Laura herself.

Duane notices, opts out and stares at his legal pad.

Gregg, wrapping his arms around himself, his eyes closed, rocks back and forth in a stupor, "And, by the way, Brian's not my friend."

After a few seconds of silence, Duane stands, pats Gregg's arm. Seeing that, Laura also stands to leave. Gregg remains slouched over on the table and starts to sob again. He doesn't acknowledge they're about to depart.

"I'll file this missing person's report and alert people in the area to keep a lookout for her. I'll also notify the state Fish and Game about your wolves. For right now, that's about all we can do," Duane says in a soothing tone.

Just as they are about to walk out the cabin door, Duane adds, "And, oh, yes, did she take clothes or other belongings with her?"

Gregg gestures to a coat hook by the door where a worn-out leather purse hangs.

"Nope. Even left her purse and glasses here."

Visibly grimacing at hearing Gregg's words, an uneasy feeling that Evie may never be found alive sends chills down Laura's spine.

43

Sit-down Standoff

Laura and Duane sit angrily at the kitchen table in her cabin, untouched wine and snacks in front of them. As they talk, their voices continue to rise until they're both angry, shouting.

Duane's face is red. Laura looks sullen. Their arms are folded towards one another in an I'm-not-budging standoff.

"I was there! You weren't! I saw the two of them interact together. Brian was repulsed by Evie. She was smelly and dirty and obsessed with those filthy wolves she was almost French kissing! She totally grossed him out! Period!"

Laura pauses briefly to take a breath, then announces, "She smelled like wolf shit! Not like someone you'd want go to bed with! Bottom line? I think Gregg's either killed her or is holding her hostage."

The veins in Duane's neck bulge.

"Bullshit! Timing's just too coincidental! Remember, this is my profession, my business. I investigate crimes!"

She's unmoved; she turns her head to face the wall on her right, refusing to look at him.

Duane takes a breath and continues, "I can clearly see that Gregg is completely innocent! Evie has run away with Brian! End of story!"

Her voice gets louder, her face contorts and her anger spills over. She screams at Duane, her eyes disappearing, as her lids form slits.

"And I've spent four years as an investigative reporter, and it's also my business to observe things objectively! I saw their relationship! She may have wanted to leave with him, but he wasn't interested. And Gregg was jealous as hell. If looks could kill," she stops and her voice becomes shrill and overly loud, "she'd be dead by now, which she probably already is!"

Destiny, upset by the shouting, starts to pace as if she wants out of there. She trots to the cabin door, asking to be let outside. Neither of them moves; dead silence prevails.

Then Duane's words suddenly shoot out. He stands, hands on his hips. "I gotta get back and write my report."

He pivots, heads for the door, his back to her. Laura remains seated. Saying nothing, she waves good-riddance, dismissing him with the sweep of her hand.

As she hears his car door slam shut, the engine start and the car peel out, she stands and stares at herself in the window's reflection. Her face looks distorted and angry.

44

Riding Solo

As the beaver pond comes into view, Laura starts directing guests with words and gestures about where they should tie their horses and where to obtain drinks and snacks.

She dismounts and ties Solo to a tree. She routinely assists a group of older guests dismounting. She distributes the drinks and food, but seems half-hearted in her efforts. The guests chat, stroll around, take photos. Destiny runs back and forth. Laura fails to react when two Magpies swoop down and land nearby. One young boy tosses them some treats. They devour the snacks as he tries to take a photo. Chipmunks scamper begging for handouts.

An explosion of automatic gunfire suddenly rips through the area. People and horses jump in unison. Laura eyes the trail to Los Lobos Cabin. A man in his 40s who introduced himself to her earlier as Al Hill, looks furious.

He spits out his words, "Christ Almighty! I left Detroit to get away from guns. What the hell?"

He looks at Laura for answers.

"Don't know, but I don't like it!" she says to the group, "I think we'd better all high-tail it back to the ranch. Sorry folks."

A red-haired middle-aged woman looks as if she alone has special insight on what has just taken place. She talks to her husband in a confidential tone but loud enough for others to hear. She maintains an all-knowing smile while the other guests seem clearly shaken.

"They do this on purpose to try to make it seem like the old west. You just wait and see. It's fake, part of the dude-ranch experience," she states emphatically.

Some of the guests overhear her.

Not reassured by her pronouncements, the shaky group remounts and heads down the trail. Everyone except the red-haired woman keeps checking their backs. She continues to look smug.

Laura uses the ranch's mobile telephone. Her tone is urgent.

"Jerry? Come in."

Jerry drops his hay rake, turns down his music and answers, "Whatcha need, Laura?"

"Just heard shots, sounded like an automatic, coming from Los Lobos Cabin," Laura spills out rapidly. "We're heading back to the ranch."

"Ever'body okay?"

"Just shaken up a bit."

"I'll let Vince know and we'll get hold of Duane."

45

Night Riders

Three large wolves silhouetted by the bright moonlight slink stealthily through the woods. They move as one, night riders on the wind.

The sleeping lamb on the edge of the pasture, lying at its mother's side, never sees nor hears them approach. The mother sheep's mouth continues to moves slowly as she chews softly, her eyes barely open.

The kill takes little effort once the Alpha male pounces on the lamb and fatally punctures its neck in a single split-second act. The sudden movement causes the remainder of the flock to jump to their feet and stand alert. They do not react as the three wolves rip and tear at the lamb, running away with various parts in their jaws.

Once back inside their den, the pack vigorously pulls at and then devours what remains of the lamb carcass, separating the flesh from its wool and skin. After their meal, when all of the wolves lie down together, their bodies touching and overlapping, the pups happily tumble over the backs of satiated and snoring adults before finding a sleeping place.

Soon the den is again still, silent.

46

Curtain Call

Keith scans Laura's groceries. The general store is empty, and he realizes he alone has Laura's undivided attention. Excited about the day's gossip, he is eager to talk.

"Hear there was some shootin' up your way. Duane was in here when he got the word. Left right away."

Leery of getting into it with Keith, she utters a non-committal, "Yeah. I have a real bad feeling about what's happened."

"Ya think old Greggo did hisself in?"

She tries to sound nonchalant, but finds herself talking too much, another throw-back to often being the first person to learn about crimes, natural disasters and political news before reports are heard on radio or television stations or appear as front-page articles in newspapers. She still likes having the inside scoop and telling her friends, neighbors and relatives the details about what has just taken place.

"Don't know what to think. He was pretty upset and drunk when we saw him. We'll just have to wait and see," she says immediately regretting her over-talking. "Thanks, Keith, gotta go."

She picks up her bag of groceries, walks out the door to her car, puts the bags in the trunk, stops, then suddenly heads back inside the store.

Already in the back room, Keith can been seen through the center opening in the thin curtain. A blurry naked female form is on the screen. Hearing the store door opening again, he quickly clicks off the set and emerges from behind the curtain, his face flushed, looking surprised to see Laura return.

"Question, Keith, do you know where I could rent a DVD on wolves? A documentary?"

"Um. Yep. Right over there on that shelf. Gregg, um, ordered 'em. Kept 'em for months. Nobody else ever asks for 'em."

He walks quickly to the shelf on one side of the store and after a few seconds returns with two dusty video cassettes. He wipes them on his jeans and hands them to Laura, lightly brushing her hand as he releases them.

She pulls away and frowns, saying nothing. "Can't use these old things. Don't have a VCR. Thanks for looking."

She starts to leave, placing them back on the counter.

"The ranch has two or three old VCRs with headsets for guests to use in the main lounge. Dudes rent cassettes down here all the time. Jerry'll let you use the machine for nothin'," Keith says. "Just bring 'em back sometime. No charge, for *you*."

"Thanks," she says walking away with them, not looking at Keith.

Keith, staring at her as she walks away, sighs and turns around to resurrect the nude on his screen.

47

Obscured View

At her laptop, Laura sits forward reading a long, small-print article. She stops, rubs her eyes, then continues. She picks up her cell phone and selects auto-dial.

Answering on the first ring, Duane mumbles, "Armstrong."

"Got a second?"

"Yep, what's up?"

"I dug up some facts online that may explain Gregg's behavior. Can I read you a paragraph of this medical article?"

"Sure," he says, sounding only mildly interested.

Laura scrolls back to the beginning of the article and asks, "Remember I told you that the doctor on the trail ride told me she'd read research that drugs and alcohol up here above timberline have some odd effects? Well, listen to this."

She reads to him: "Tests have sometimes shown that alcohol or marijuana or other substances such as methamphetamines can be enhanced when used at high altitudes, above 10,000 feet, and cause the user to become abnormally affected by smaller amounts than at sea level."

"So what's your point?" Duane asks, unimpressed. "We already know he was stoned; we just don't know exactly how much weed he smoked or how much Jack Daniels he drank. Doesn't really matter!"

"Just thought you'd like to know," Laura says, somewhat chagrined.

"Well, now I do. That all?"

"Yes," she answers, "Night."

"Night," Duane says.

She doesn't see him shake his head, smirk or look oddly at his cell phone as he clicks off.

48

Special Delivery

Standing in front of the store's customer-rented mailboxes, Keith examines a letter. The envelope is open, as if it were never sealed. He looks around to be sure nobody is watching, slips the letter out and begins to read it quietly to himself, his lips moving noticeably.

The paper is wrinkled and smudged with fingerprints. It looks as if it has been typed on a typewriter, its individual letters inked erratically

Dear Evie.

Our reunion was great. Thank you for making my visit memorable. Seeing you, the wolves and the videos reminded me that part of me will be always with you forever. Take care of our precious Alaskan jewels.

Love you, Brian

He quickly inserts the letter back into the unsealed envelope and places it into one of the numbered boxes.

As soon as Duane comes in to ask for his own mail, Keith retrieves it and takes out the letter addressed to Evie as well. He tries to appear cool as if he's serving Duane a subpoena. He slaps the envelope into Duane's hand while raising his eyebrows in a visual code-like manner. "Interesting!" he whispers.

Reading the Los Lobos Cabin address and seeing Evie's name piques Duane's interest. Noticing the envelope is unsealed, he immediately looks suspiciously at Keith, who raises both his hands as if to say, "Not me! Didn't do it!"

Duane reads the letter. It's dated the day Evie vanished. He holds the envelope up to his nose and sniffs it. "This thing reeks of cigarettes, or maybe pot, too."

Keith again tries to look innocent.

"It isn't even signed or sealed. How'd you get this? Anybody could have written this. Fingerprints would probably be easy to trace, assuming there are more than just yours on this."

Concerned, Keith begins to explain, "Honest, Duane, it was here with the rest of the mail in the bag when I got here this morning."

He gestures toward the large U.S. Postal Service canvas bag on the floor.

"Somebody coulda put the letter in there. Sometimes the mail truck drops the bags off real early in the morning and leaves them sittin' outside the front door. People have even gone through it and gotten their own mail out before I open up the store!"

Duane does not respond at first and then appears to be talking to himself.

"I guess this means I get to make another trip up to see the wolf man," he says, keeping the envelope and starting to return to his patrol car.

"This here's for Los Lobos Cabin, too. You might as well take these along," Keith says, handing him some mail and placing it in a paper bag with handles.

Duane seals the envelope and puts it into the paper bag, grabs a candy bar, tosses a dollar on the counter and exits without further comment.

49

Band of Brothers

Cumulus clouds tower over Los Lobos Cabin. Gregg stands on the porch and lets out a shrieking howl. Waits. Listens. Howls again. He plops down on the stairs and sobs. He swigs from a beer bottle and howls again, this time a pitiful, mournful sound.

The sky opens up and drowns the area.

Drenched and cold, Gregg remains on the stairs. The sky turns darker; lightning flashes.

From Gregg's perspective on the stairs, Timberline Ranch's 4x4 suddenly slides into fuzzy view. It stops. Rain continues to pour. Duane in his sheriff's rain slicker and boots exits and slogs up the stairs toward Gregg who sits immobilized, looking as if he wants to move; he cannot.

Duane walks up to him, pats his shoulder and yells into the wind. "Hey, partner. Let's get outta this stuff."

Gregg struggles, stands unsteadily. He barely acknowledges Duane who lifts him under his armpits to a standing position.

"What's the fuckin' difference?" Gregg blurts.

"Listen, buddy, I know what you're goin' through. Let's go inside and talk."

Duane helps him across the porch and opens the door.

Once inside, Duane says cheerfully, "Got some mail here for ya."

He hands the damp paper bag to Gregg who tosses it recklessly onto the spool table. One newspaper-sized advertisement slides out and onto the floor.

Gregg slowly growls, "Shhhhhit. Whada I care?"

"Thought there might something in your mail to shed light on why Evie left or where she's ended up."

Gregg dumps the bag's contents out and makes a half-hearted scan of the envelopes, picking out the letter with Evie's name on it and ripping it open.

Rain pounds the roof.

"Maybe," he says, squinting and holding the letter at arm's length to get it into focus.

A lightning strike knocks out the power and the room goes dark.

Gregg holds the letter toward the window and reads it, then hands it to Duane who acts as if he's seeing it for the first time.

"Hmmm. Guess that kinda rules out her leaving with him, huh?"

Gregg sounds bitter. His speech is slurred, "Bet she wrote it herself. Be just like her. What a dreamer!"

Duane frowns.

Gregg takes a deep breath and blurts out, "That bastard Brian is nuts, though. Wouldn't put anything past him, either. He's hated me since I stole Evie from him. He'd love to destroy me. Maybe he wrote this to throw us off."

Duane doesn't react, although he listens to Gregg's analysis and feels it has some credibility at first. Then putting it through the filter of Gregg's alcohol and marijuana level, he immediately discounts anything he's just heard.

Power returns to the cabin.

Duane spots rolling papers and pot in baggies on the table. "Say, guy, think you gotta face facts. She's gone. Left. Kaput!"

No response from Gregg who hangs his head.

"Once when I was really bummed out, a friend told me that sometimes you gotta bury your past. Bury it and just move on," Duane continues without success to try to engage him.

The two sit in silence. Duane looks at the pot again, stands, pats Gregg on the back and heads for the door. The rain is still heavy. Duane hurries down the cabin stairs as Gregg stands and watches him from the window. Duane passes a planter containing what he instantly recognizes as healthy, now-soggy marijuana plants. He hesitates, turns his head, squats down and looks closely at them before proceeding to the ranch's vehicle.

50

Timberline Trauma

Rain clouds are being carried away by a brisk wind. The dudes and Jerry wear plastic ponchos as they ride horses near the beaver pond. Suddenly, gunshots again echo through the area.

The horses are startled; one rears up, almost dumping his rider onto the ground.

Everyone stares uphill toward the direction of the sounds, Los Lobos Cabin. Jerry frowns and squints as the shots repeat. Everyone looks to him for direction.

Without hesitation, Jerry announces, "Folks, maybe we'll just head right back the same way we came, instead of finishin' the loop. Sounds like somebody might be doin' some target practice up yonder. Don't want us to end up the targets."

Upset, he picks up his mobile phone to make another unwelcomed call to Vince while turning his horse around and leading the group downhill. They follow him nervously looking back over their shoulders from time to time until the ranch comes back into view.

51

Heard the Earth Move

Like someone doing a challenging jigsaw puzzle, Laura has put several pieces of information together that convince her Evie didn't merely run away.

When she objectively steps back, though, she realizes some key pieces are definitely still missing, and she needs to locate them.

Also, nothing fits exactly right.

She returns to the hill overlooking Los Lobos Cabin to see for herself if Gregg can provide anything to help reveal a more complete picture. Destiny is back locked in Laura's cabin, Solo is tied securely to a tree, and Duane is on duty elsewhere. She has come to the conclusion that she alone must take the time to do what she can to find Evie.

The rain has left the grass slippery on the hillside. Her riding boots are not suited for hiking on the wet slope and she loses her footing several times, falling onto her hands. As she continues to climb, she becomes winded and stops frequently to catch her breath. Just as she starts upward again, she abruptly stops as she instantly recognizes the sound of heavy earth-moving equipment.

Stunned to hear the noise so close by, she has a gut feeling that she may be closer to finding that key puzzle piece.

Topping the hill she lies forward in the wet weeds and peers down, using her binoculars.

She adjusts the binoculars and focuses on Gregg operating a bright yellow Caterpillar backhoe, digging a huge hole in the ground a few yards from the bottom of the stairs, near the parking area.

Laura gasps and feels weak in the knees, lying completely prone to try to recover. She leans forward to watch again. She pictures Evie being buried alive.

Mud and rocks fall from the sides of the steel bucket as Gregg backs up and dumps another load onto an already large mound of wet dirt. The backhoe's motor dominates. Gregg's eyes look like a wild man's as he continues to work feverishly, much of his long wet hair bursting out of the ponytail and stringing down his face.

She stares transfixed for more than 20 minutes as he digs, dumps, fills, smoothes.

Finally, she decides to walk downhill towards him and begins waving, trying to get his attention. He is focused, driven. He does not see her approaching. The noise of the backhoe drowns out everything.

When she gets within 10 feet of him, he sees movement and is clearly startled. He brakes the machine and jumps off, backing away, almost as if disassociating himself from it. It continues to run in neutral.

He slogs almost frantically through the mud towards her. He seems taken aback and immediately attempts to explain himself. He shouts in one long sentence, "Um, oh, I had to do this work we have garbage and wolf shit, you know it has to be, um, buried I hadn't done it for a while."

Laura says nothing. The longer she is silent, the more he talks.

"Had to do it when the rain, er, stopped and all," he says, fumbling in his shirt pocket for a cigarette. He pulls out a joint instead and lights it.

"No worries. I just want to ask you a couple questions, if it's okay," Laura says in an overly slow, calm manner.

Gregg, breathless and unfriendly, smokes, "Fine. Let's, um, ah, go inside."

He returns to the back hoe and turns off its motor.

For a split second, Laura's logical side of her brain takes over and she considers what she's doing. If, indeed, Gregg may be a wife abuser at best and a murderer at worst, why would she agree to go inside a remote cabin with him while he's smoking pot? Then, her emotional side takes over and she vows to locate Evie at all costs. Remembering the two people who never gave up on her, she follows Gregg up the steep stairs trying not to blow this opportunity to find out what he knows or what he's done.

On the porch, he removes his muddy boots. In the process, he drops the joint and it lands in a puddle.

"Shit!" he says, kicking it away with his bare feet and walking into the cabin.

She scrapes her boots on the edges of the stairs but continues inside, still tracking mud. She sits on one of the metal chairs at the spool table and stares uncomfortably at a rifle and an automatic handgun resting beside it, along with ammunition. Gregg places the weapons on the floor. The bullets remain.

He steps over to the refrigerator, opens it and reaches for a beer bottle. He pops the cap easily and it falls to the floor. He kicks it away. He doesn't ask Laura if she wants anything, just sits down with her.

She observes that he is clearly rattled as he takes long pulls on the beer then folds his hands on the table like a truant school kid ready to hear his punishment.

"So, okay. Ask away."

"I still think there might be an explanation for Evie's disappearance. I was wondering if she's involved in any animal-rights organizations or anything like that?"

"Nope!" Gregg says emphatically, pulling again on his beer.

"I was on the Internet last night and I saw several organizations that are either for or against reintroducing of wolves to Yellowstone National Park," she says.

"So what? Evie wasn't involved with that shit, but," he stands, puts down his beer and walks quickly to the next room.

From her vantage point, Laura can see a computer and printer. Next to it on a table relatively free of debris is an ancient typewriter like her grandmother had in her attic. It holds a piece of paper. She wonders if Gregg has used the relic to write his books on the Yupiks.

He returns holding a dozen or more sheets of paper, tosses them down in front of her and resumes drinking his beer. After a couple of gulps, he says, "Check these out. She's been emailing a lady whose been asking lots of questions 'bout our wolves. I glanced at 'em. The bitch is nuts."

Again Laura feels confused as to which woman he is referring. She picks up the papers, taps them on the tabletop to straighten them and tries to speed read them.

"Mind if I take these and try to make sense out of them?" she asks politely, looking for eye contact with him.

"Whatever," Gregg shrugs, looking away, finishing his beer, and going for another. He comes back to the table and continues to stand uncomfortably close to her.

"That all you need?"

"For now, thanks," Laura answers, eager to leave the cabin and Gregg's sight.

52

Happy Ending

Duane reads a paperback romance novel as he lies on his couch. His cell phone rings. He looks annoyed, puts down the book.

"Yep?" he says, glancing to see who's calling.

"Hi. I've found something I'd like to show you," Laura says.

"What's up?"

"I started going over some emails Gregg let me see early today. Seems Evie has been in touch with an animal activist gal named Lynda Koehler. Big deal with the Yellowstone wolf reintroduction effort."

"Really? Want to meet for a bite to eat at Crystal's and talk about it?" he says, sounding more interested than he has before when hearing her ideas.

"Yeah. When?" Laura says. "I can be there in 30 minutes, can you?"

"See you there," Duane says, hanging up.

A half hour later when she walks in, Duane is already at their back booth. Laura doesn't even sit down before she begins to chatter, "I did some checking and there's a website all about that Koehler lady if you want to go online and check it out."

"Yeah? So?" Duane looks skeptical.

She shuffles through several papers and stops at one.

"Seems she wants Gregg and Evie to release their wolves back into the wild. Maybe we need to locate her. Maybe that's where Evie went when she abandoned her Jeep that night. Maybe took the wolves to the lady and they're going to release them."

Duane immediately dismisses her theory, "Sounds unlikely. How do you transport that many wolves?"

"Well, I already found her phone number. Called. No answer."

Duane sits up and leans forward. He looks somewhat peeved and his tone changes from friendly to clearly annoyed. He frowns.

"Ya know, you're really something else!" he doesn't elaborate, but she gleans he's not amused.

She continues anyway. "I also found that in some of Evie's emails to her she keeps using the same Yupik word."

"You peek? Huh?" Duane says, making a face,

Laura is talking a mile a minute and his eyes show he is giving up trying to follow her train of thought.

"Yupik. It's the language of the Yupik Eskimos in Alaska where Evie, Brian and Gregg taught school. Anyway, the word is 'amorak.'"

"What the hell are you talking about, Laura? You're not making sense and you're hyper. I don't need to go on any wild-goose chases!"

Laura ignores his comment and begins to spell the word to him, "A, M, O, R, A, K. In her emails, Evie keeps saying she is losing her amorak and needs to get it back."

"And?" he asks cynically.

"I've been online for a couple hours and finally found a Yupik elder to explain it to me. He says amorak literally is sometimes used as their word for lone wolf, one who leaves the pack and hunts alone, but it is also often used to mean spirit of the wolf. "

As she speaks, she picks up what appears to be a recent color copy from a computer printer showing a close-up of a gray wolf looking directly into the camera, its almond-shaped eyes mystical, spiritual. She hands it to Duane who looks at it and immediately tosses it back down onto the table.

"So what? How does this shit help us find Evie?" Duane sounds increasingly frustrated.

"The Yupik guy said their people use the word alone to describe a person who needs to escape into nature in order to find his own spirit."

"Laura, what does all this mean?" he states rather than asks.

"Duane, don't you see? I think Evie may have gone with the Koehler woman to find herself."

Duane's cell phone goes off. He checks it, stands and says, "Sorry. This is important. Gotta go!"

Laura looks out the picture window to see the flashing lights of Duane's patrol car in the parking lot.

"Shit!" she says to herself, picking up the papers and stuffing all but one of them into her purse as she stands up and storms past Crystal who has just shown up with two glasses of water and two menus. The wolf photo lies face-up on the floor near the booth.

Crystal sees it, puts down the menus and water glasses, picks it up and examines it, looking puzzled.

53

Wolf Cries

In the moonlight, several adult wolves and pups trot through a pasture in total silence. Suddenly they stop. Then two adult wolves begin to stalk calves lying near their mothers. In a split second there is a flurry of activity, an obvious kill.

Cows and calves scatter.

Again silence.

A large adult wolf drags a newborn calf over to the waiting pack. Joyful howling erupts.

On the other side of the foothills near the Bar S Ranch on River Road, three young men sit in a pickup pulled off to the shoulder. They drink beer and toss their empties out into the ditch parallel to them.

Out of nowhere, a full-grown wolf approaches the driver's side of the truck. It stands on its hind legs and places its front paws on the frame of the open window. Its ears flatten and its tail is down in the submissive position. The wolf then utters a soft whimper similar to a dog seeking affection. Its amber eyes are in a fixed stare at the driver.

The startled driver grabs a rifle from the gun rack behind his seat, cocks it and aims it at the wolf. He fires point blank, the blast knocking the wolf nearly four feet back before it falls heavily to the ground, its chest now a huge bloody cavity.

Within 15 minutes, a flashing bar of red lights atop a sheriff's patrol car can be seen speeding through Big Timber heading toward River Road and the Bar S turnoff.

54

Coping with Cops

Jerry and Laura curry the horses in the corral as the sun comes up. The barn lights are on. She is antsy, clearly unable to control her curiosity.

He's more matter-of-fact, "Duane wouldn't tell me much of anything when he got back from Gregg's."

She commiserates, "Me neither. Cops! Ugh! Gave me the old 'just-the-facts-ma'am' routine."

Jerry laughs, "And, ma'am, just what are the facts?"

"Let's compare notes," Laura says. "You first."

"He told me Gregg was stoned. Found a ton of pot growing in his front yard. Thinks he probably has lots stashed, too, since they have their own greenhouse."

She looks surprised, realizing she too had been to the cabin twice but never noticed marijuana growing anywhere.

"So, I guess he'll arrest him?"

"Don't actually know. He didn't say, or at least didn't say nothin' to me."

55

Coffee Klatch

Keith and Laura sit in a booth at Crystal's. She faces the door, not listening to Keith's banter which continues as Duane comes in.

"...and anyways the kid dropped his sister's math book down the hole in the outhouse and..."

Duane locks eyes with Laura and smiles. It has been two days since he walked out on her and she has wondered if he would even agree to meet her when she called to ask him.

He looks happy to see her and interrupts Keith in mid-sentence.

"So, Miss investigative reporter, got your call. What is it *this* time?" Duane says, smiling, as he sits next to Keith and gives Laura his undivided attention. As she starts to talk, she notices him staring into her eyes and completely focusing on her.

She looks anxious to tell what she knows. She sits forward.

"Okay, I'll admit I was snooping again, but, well, I couldn't help myself. I rode Solo up to their cabin again after the rain stopped."

Duane interrupts, "Better watch out, Missie. He's been known to shoot at strange noises."

Laura gives him a drop-dead look and continues in a confidential whisper, "Yeah, right. Anyway, you won't believe what I saw him doing."

Both Duane and Keith lean forward, eager to hear.

56

Starry, Starry Night

It is past 8 p.m. The cabin is crowded with still-unopened boxes left from move-in day. Dirty dinner dishes fill the sink. Laura is on the couch with her lap-top open on the coffee table with the Frontier Airlines homepage on its screen. She has her cell phone in her hand and a determined look on her face.

"Please confirm if the passenger whose name I gave you was on your flight 104 from Bozeman to Denver. It is urgent that I contact her," she says into the cell phone.

"No, I'm not a family member. I'm a journalist working with her family to try to locate her."

Shutting down the computer, she waits for the dark screen, stands and walks outside with the phone at her ear. Destiny follows.

Laura and Destiny sit on the porch steps. Several minutes have passed and she has not gotten her answer. Frustrated, she clicks off the cell phone and puts it into her pants pocket when she sees Duane's patrol car pull up.

As he exits the car his radio phone crackles. He stops and listens as a call comes in. He shakes his head, signaling to Laura that it's not for him, clicks off the radio phone and walks toward her, smiling.

After a quick hug for each other and a rub for Destiny, the three begin to walk down the dirt path toward the lake. Laura and Duane meander around the lake. Destiny sniffs and happily races around. The crescent moon is mirrored in the water and reflected stars create a romantic and beautiful scene, which is not lost on them. They hold hands and stroll along the water's edge.

A lone wolf howls in the distance. They stop abruptly and look at each other. Duane tries to discount the howl's seriousness by merely shrugging his shoulders.

"God that's so eerie! Wonder where Evie is tonight? Sounds like the wolf is mourning for her," Laura says.

"Sounds more like your local garden-variety coyote to me."

Laura shakes her head, sighs, "Right."

He disengages his hand from hers and turns to face her, folding his arms and looking at her with total seriousness.

"Listen, Laura, I know you want to believe Gregg is some sort of ax murderer pervert, but we have no evidence of that. Zero! He's just an average weirdo whose wife ditched him. That's the long and short of it."

It becomes a stare-down and she's not blinking nor backing off.

"Duane, you gotta give that up! You're doing what my psyche prof at college used to call selective perception—seeing what you want to see and ignoring obvious facts. It's also called the cry-wolf syndrome."

He immediately snaps back, "And you aren't doing the same thing at all, right? You think every man you see wants to kill his wife!"

Their voices rise in contrast to the serenity of the scene.

"Mine is the only logical explanation we have right now and it's based on the facts, Laura."

"Speaking of facts, I emailed the airline and did a follow-up call to see if Evie took that flight Brian was on from Bozeman. Told them I was a journalist working with the family of a missing woman and needed to find her. Haven't heard back."

Duane kicks the dirt in frustration as his tone turns sarcastic, "Right. And she's just gonna get on a flight using her real name too? Wouldn't she maybe, just maybe use a fake I.D., huh? She left her purse at home and didn't have her real I.D.!"

Neither of them speaks for a while. They turn to head back toward the path to the cabin.

She will not let him have the last word and she blurts out, "By the way, I assume you've also figured out why Gregg was digging that big deep hole in front of their cabin. Making a swimming pool was he?"

Duane becomes even more annoyed. He speaks in a slow, overly controlled and patronizing manner.

Laura sulks.

"He needed to dig the hole because they bury their garbage and don't believe in unnecessary burning. Environmentalists. Duh! Get it?"

Laura continues to say nothing.

"And I believe him!" Duane adds emphatically.

Laura smirks, rolls her eyes and smacks her lips in disgust, "How do we know it's garbage and not Evie he's buried?"

As she utters the words, Laura gets a far-away look.

Duane notices her not continuing the argument as her eyes seem to glaze over.

"What I mean is, Laura, sometimes there is a good explanation for people's behavior," he says less angrily.

It is night in Texas at the cemetery. From inside the metal box, she hears Al, then another man, grunting, straining.

"Are you listening, Laura?"

She returns to the present and barks out harshly, "I heard you, Duane! Gregg's gone green. Sure! And Al was just recycling me, too, you probably think?"

He snaps back, "You've completely forgotten what the word objectivity means! You call yourself a reporter?"

She counters, "You've got plenty of your own baggage! Not good for a cop either! But worse than baggage, you're just plain naive!"

A shrill, close-in wolf chorus interrupts them. They turn, look at each other and then proceed to walk back to the cabin in silence. He gets into his patrol car; she and Destiny walk to the cabin's front door. Neither looks at the other. Duane drives off.

Later in the evening with the cabin's windows open and all the lights out, the moon and stars provide ample illumination inside. Laura sits on the couch watching a DVD on her laptop. Destiny lies at her feet. The room around her is a total wreck. When the on-screen wolves howl, Destiny's ears perk up.

"Don't worry. They're really not here, girl."

Then Laura looks out the window into the darkness, almost as if to verify her own comment.

On the top of the coffee table illuminated by moonlight is a CD sleeve with a handwritten note, "Here's the wolf DVDs I promised. Had them copied from cassettes. Thanks for helping out and taking such good care of my Solo."

It's signed, "Vince."

57

Collateral Damage

Inside the corral, Jerry and Laura prepare horses for a breakfast ride. Duane drives up in his patrol car and pulls in next to the fence.

He gets out. "Mornin'," he says to them both and then asks Jerry, "Say, has the ranch lost any calves the last few days?"

"Not that I know of but there were still a couple cows ready to calf in our south pasture. All the others calved after the last big snows. Don't know if anyone's checked on 'em."

"Trouble?" Laura asks.

"Bar S thinks wolves got to two of their youngest calves. Called in a report in the middle of the night."

She grimaces.

"Nothing much left but bits of their hide and soft hooves. Bob Johnson's really pissed."

"That's a good 20 miles away. Can't be them hippies' wolves," Jerry says to Duane.

Laura interrupts before Duane has a chance to respond. She sounds authoritative, "Actually, wolves can travel more than that, sometimes even up to 40 miles in one night of hunting."

Duane's tone instantly becomes arrogant and nasty. "So now you're the world's greatest authority on wolves, too?"

Her mood sours and she scowls at him.

Jerry looks uncomfortable, ducks down to check a saddle cinch and lays low.

Laura drops the curry comb into the dirt, leaves it and marches from the corral.

When she's out of sight, Jerry peeks over the horse's back at Duane, teasing with his words.

"Now we know one thing for sure. Bob Johnson's not the only one pissed!"

"Damned know-it-all women!" Duane says as he kicks the dirt and stomps back to the patrol car.

58

Mighty Hunters

It's early afternoon. Keith, along with Tim and Larry, two cowboys in their 20s, and several older bystanders with children crowd around a dirty pickup in front of the general store, peering into its bed.

A closer view reveals Tundra's body with a huge wound to her chest area. The three men look excited and mystified as they discuss the kill and display their bloody trophy. Everyone is talking at once and some people take photos with their cell phones.

"So, where did ya kill it?" one bystander asks. "Better not be over inside Yellowstone! Got a permit?"

"Nah, it was over here by the Bar S." Tim says. "It's a female."

"We think she belonged to them hippies living up above Timberline Ranch property," Keith adds, "Weird how it happened."

"Shit, yeah, it was! We was just sittin' in the truck havin' a couple beers and she come up to us, almost like she wanted to be fed," Larry says. "Wasn't nothin' like them wolves we seen in Yellowstone last summer over in Lamar Valley or in Hayden. Them was real spooky. They put their heads down and slinked away from us real fast like. It was at night, too, but they didn't want nothin' to do with us at all!"

He continues, "But, this one almost was tame or somethin'. It scared us shitless, so I grabbed the thirty-thirty from the rack and blasted her as she stood there. At first, I thought she was gonna jump right into the cab of the truck!"

"Scared the crap out of me, too!" Tim adds.

"Yeah, when she come up to us, she looked more like a dog would act. Kinda wagged her tail and sorta whined."

"But she just kept on a comin' and lookin' at us with them gold eyes!" Keith says, seeming frightened again as he recalls the scene.

The men continue to talk excitedly about the kill, their comments blending together.

"Larry shot her point blank."

"There's a big fine for killin' a wolf without a license!" a teenager says in an authoritative voice. "I read it's a hundred thousand unless you can prove it was killin' your livestock."

Larry shakes his head. He's annoyed and is tiring of the conversation.

"No, no. You're talkin' 'bout the gray wolf; them used to be endangered. Not now, though, and not this here kind, either."

"A wolf's a wolf last time I checked," Keith says.

They continue to examine the massive wound in Tundra's side and chest.

Larry raises Tundra's head, opens her mouth to show her teeth. The group, as one, takes a step back from the dead wolf.

"I got me a book back at the house. This here's an Arctic wolf. Definitely."

"Ya better hope so. You're up shit's creek if it ain't."

59

Makin' Up

Duane is on his office land-line telephone. It's 7 a.m. He punches in a number. After a few seconds, he sounds as if he's speaking to a machine.

"Listen, Laura, I really apologize. You didn't deserve that. I was a jerk. I realize what you've been through in your life, and you didn't need to have me insult you like that in front of Jerry. I'm just so frustrated with this case and don't know exactly where to go with it. But I am really sorry. Truly. I've been up most of the night waiting for it to be an okay time to call you. Now you're not home."

Laura stands over her land-line phone and answering machine and monitors the voicemail as she hears Duane's words. The cabin is still a wreck, dirty dishes, newspapers everywhere.

The answering machine records most of Duane's message and then she picks up.

Her tone is icy. "Oh, hello, Officer Armstrong."

"Hi, Laura. Sorry about blowing up at you. You really got dumped on. Not your fault.

Laura doesn't respond.

Duane continues to sound contrite, "I just think this whole thing is weird. Evie's missing, Gregg's freaked out and the wolves are having a banquet at our ranchers' expense. Got me really stressed. Don't have a wife to yell at anymore or a dog to kick, so you got the whole load. Sorry."

Laura waits for a few seconds and finally speaks.

"Well, I acted like a big jerk, too. I don't have anybody but Destiny to talk to, and as long as I feed her she doesn't ever tell me I'm out of line."

"Does that mean we're still friends?" he asks.

Laura waits a second or two. Then answers softly, "Sure."

"You up for some company? Actually I need your opinion on something."

Her sarcasm returns, her voice reveals her smile as she speaks, "Oh, really now. You want *my* opinion?"

Duane laughs, too, "Yeah, really!"

"Sorry, couldn't help myself," Laura says and adds, "Sure, come on up."

An hour later, Duane sits on the side of her bed in his underwear. He starts to get dressed. Laura lies shoulders bare with a sheet covering her. She seems relaxed and content.

"By the way, what was it you wanted my opinion on?"

Duane smiles at her, "I just wondered if you thought making up was going to be as much fun as I imagined."

Laura grins at him. He pulls her close.

60

News at 11

The television is on in her cabin. Laura ignores it. She's sorting through some moving boxes still stacked throughout the living room. When she hears the news bulletin, she drops everything and races over, turning up the sound.

The voice of Bozeman newscaster Karen Gilbert is heard:

"Possibly a dozen or more Arctic wolves may be on the loose near Timberline Ranch in the Crazy Mountains near Big Timber. Cattlemen in the area report livestock killed. Rancher Bob Johnson joins us live from the Bar S Ranch."

A close-up of Johnson, his barn in the background, fills the screen.

"Tell us what you know, Mr. Johnson."

Johnson, a grizzled cowboy who has smoked too many cigarettes and ridden horses too long in the high-altitude sun, is in his late 50s. He sports a stained hat and a grim look.

"Dozen wolves have escaped. We believe they're owned by a couple who brought 'em down secretly from Alaska a few years back."

The reporter continues, "And you're convinced that two of your calves were killed by wolves?"

"Sure as I'm standin' here. There's nothin' much left of whatever a wolf gets a holt of."

"Mr. Johnson, have you notified authorities?"

Johnson nods his head. His tone is harsh and cynical. "Yep, but so far nothin's been done. That's the government for ya. Fish and Game and the Sheriff's Department are all out lookin' for 'em, or, so they say."

Gilbert asks a final question, "Maybe it's a bad time to ask, but how do you feel about wolves that were reintroduced to Yellowstone a few years back, Mr. Johnson?"

He tilts his head, narrows his eyes, takes a deep breath and spits out his words.

"Well, we was told to support the reintroduction program because we didn't have no wolves up here no more. Now it's out of control and the state's gotta pass out huntin' licenses to kill them. We don't have no dinosaurs up here no more either. Anybody want them back?"

He scowls into the camera, turns and walks away.

"Thank you, Mr. Johnson."

"We also spoke earlier with the law enforcement officer who patrols the area, County Sheriff's Captain Duane Armstrong. Here's what he had to say," Gilbert says.

The live feed changes to video.

Duane sits behind his desk in the sheriff's sub-station office. He looks somewhat nervous as if he isn't filmed every day. He holds up a map of the area with one section highlighted. The camera shoots a close-up of it.

"Officer, you have highlighted the area where the missing wolves are now thought to be, is that right?" she asks. "Do you consider the escaped wolves to be a possible threat to public safety?"

"No. Not at all. There's almost no recorded attacks by wolves on people. Now, livestock is a whole other situation. We think we may have real problems in this area."

He points to the Bar S Ranch and the video portion is complete.

Laura gets close to the set.

Gilbert comes back live."This just in. KLOK has learned that a female wolf has been shot and killed near the Bar S Ranch, the exact area Deputy Armstrong has just shown our viewing audience. We'll go live now to our reporter George James in the Crazy Mountains.

James, in his 40s, holds a microphone. The camera is filming Keith, Tim and Larry as they display Tundra's bloody body in the bed of Larry's pickup. The wolf's head fills a close-up shot, its tongue hanging to one side, its amber eyes fixed.

"Which one of you shot the wolf?" James asks.

The men look nervous. No one speaks for a second or two.

Keith finally blurts out, "Larry shot 'er," pointing to Larry who raises his hand awkwardly.

"Are you aware that it is against the law to shoot a gray wolf without a permit? And do you realize the most recent hunting season has ended?" James continues.

"This here's an Arctic wolf, not one of them endangered ones."

Another close-up on the wolf's eyes as Larry says,"Besides them escaped wolves is killin' calves up here at the Bar S."

"Thank you, gentlemen." James says.

A photo of a wolf comes up on a split screen, the caption below reading, "Arctic Wolf." The dead wolf is shown beside the photo. The two look almost identical.

"Gregg Ballard, owner of the escaped wolves, has denied the dead wolf is his, although a professor from Montana State University, positively identified it as an Arctic wolf, part of a sub-species of the gray wolf, and an animal not native to our area but found in Canada, Greenland and Alaska," James states as the screen shows him back at Larry's pickup holding a microphone.

"We'll have more on this breaking story during our 11 o'clock news. Now back to you in the studio," James says.

Laura stares in disbelief at the television set and says aloud to herself, "This is awful!"

She grabs her keys and purse and heads out the door with Destiny following close behind. She forgets to put the top down and has to lower the right front window for Destiny to take up her position with her head out.

61

Learning Curve

Western music plays in the background. An instructor wearing a microphone headset leads dudes and wranglers in line dancing. Laura rushes in, scans the room for Jerry and signals him.

Everyone looks up and notices her urgency. Jerry heads for a table in the back where they sit down. Vince, looking older and more wrinkled than his late 50s, joins them.

"So, where's the fire, Laura?"

She talks a mile a minute. "Have you guys seen what's on television from Bozeman this afternoon?"

They all look surprised and shake their heads.

Jerry says, "Nope. What's up?"

"Duane's been on and so have Keith, Tim and Larry. It's about the wolf Larry shot near the Bar S," she says without taking a breath. "Vince, this thing is really escalating!"

Vince holds his head in his hands.

"Just what we didn't need! Every fuckin' bunny hugger in the country will take us on. Bet Johnson called the television stations. The bastard. Just raises cattle. He don't have to worry about the tourist business," Vince says.

Jerry and Laura look on with empathy at their friend's frustration.

Vince continues to rant. "You just know people'll cancel reservations thinkin' they're gonna get eaten by some fuckin' wolves!" He
pounds on the table. "Shit!"

A few of the dancers look over at the commotion. Seeing they
might be disturbing ranch guests, the men stand and head for the
sports bar.

There, the television blares in the background.

Vince and Jerry sit at the bar slumped over a large ashtray full of
butts. They each have half full glasses of beer.

Vince smokes.

After several minutes of silence, Vince speaks in a perturbed
tone, "I can't believe CNN has picked up the fuckin' story. Now it's
runnin' every hour. The other networks all have it, too."

Jerry shakes his head and looks into his beer for answers.

"Just can't believe what's happening!" Vince mumbles.

"They way they're carryin' on, you'd think it was a movie star
those boys shot, not somebody's pet wolf, for God's sake!" Jerry
says. "Next they'll be saying we have werewolves up here!"

Vince shakes his head, takes another pull on his beer and says
with anger, "Sue McGrath, down in Bozeman, who handles our reservations told me we got 18 cancellations already for next week. Guess
everybody in the whole fuckin' country watches fuckin' CNN!"

62

Fact or Fiction

It's afternoon. Duane sits in the ranch parking lot in his patrol car reading a new romance novel as Laura pulls up. He folds the page to mark his place, tosses the paperback onto the back seat as they exit their vehicles and pile into one of the ranch's aging pick-ups. As she gets in, she sees a large dented metal tool box directly behind the truck's cab. She tries to divert her attention from it and asks, "What the deal about you always using the ranch vehicles? I'm surprised the county allows that, insurance-wise."

Duane laughs, "The county and the ranch have an agreement that in emergencies, the sheriff's department can use their land and their vehicles. My name is personally on their insurance policies, as I hear yours is, too, for doing the trail rides."

"You're right."

"A while back the county figured out it was cheaper to use ranch vehicles and pay them back by having me supervise things like the dances and hayrides and July Fourth events than it was to purchase a new four-by or pickup. Nobody has complained and so far we haven't wrecked any of their property."

In the bed of the truck Laura sees what appears to be a large black plastic body bag with something big and heavy inside.

Suddenly her heart begins to race. She feels faint. Even though she knows it's Tundra's body, she eyes the bag and realizes it's the same size as a human and the thought sends chills down her spine.

She hears testimony from the courtroom:

"Could you detect any noises coming from the metal tool box?" the prosecuting attorney continues.

The police officer, looking as if he is reliving the moment, wipes perspiration from his brow, takes a deep breath and then continues.

"Yes we could hear something. We couldn't distinguish a voice but we heard thumping against the metal. It was surreal!"

"What happened next?"

"We used the jaws of life device to cut off the lock. Inside we saw a sheet tied with rope and a body barely moving under the sheet. We quickly got it unwrapped and inside was a woman, her mouth duct taped shut, her hands taped behind her back. She was bloody from a blow to her head and further injured from being squashed inside the box. She was near death, we felt, weak and exhausted, couldn't stand without assistance, but she was alive."

Laura snaps back to the present, takes deep breaths and consciously forces herself to think, "You're here in Montana. You're even with a cop who likes you! You're fine. This is not about you; it's about finding Evie. Not giving up on Evie."

After repeating the thoughts over and over, she begins to calm down. Duane, concentrating on his driving, doesn't notice Laura's discomfort and pulls out of the parking lot. As they drive away, Jerry waves, squats down and holds Destiny's leash, petting her and seems surprised to see Laura sitting comfortably inside a closed-in vehicle.

Duane looks like a man with a mission. He stares at the road as if he's alone. After a few miles, he breaks his silence.

"Located Brian in Chicago and talked to him today. He swears he didn't write the letter. Maybe Gregg was right. Evie probably wrote it."

Laura picks up his thought as Duane takes a breath, "Or, maybe Gregg wrote it himself to divert attention away from him."

"Hmmm. Could be. You ain't half bad as a cop, ya know?"

Laura smiles but her tone is sarcastic. "Don't try to kiss up. Too late. But, ya wanna know something?"

"Sure," Duane says, nodding his head.

"Timberline Ranch doesn't even have a typewriter, only computers. So Brian is probably telling the truth. I did spot an old one in the back room at Los Lobos Cabin, though."

Surprised, Duane smiles and gives her a thumbs-up in admiration.

The pickup bounces over the rough road and past the beaver pond. Laura again glances back sadly over her shoulder at the body bag. Then she snuggles over toward Duane.

After a few minutes, he gestures toward the bag in the truck bed.

"Anyway. Something's screwy. I just wanna watch Gregg's reaction to Brian denying the letter. And to this female wolf being shot. Probably already knows about it since it's been on television."

Laura nods her head and mumbles agreement.

"If nothing else, if he admits she's his wolf, he owes Johnson for those calves," Duane states firmly.

"Did Fish and Game perform an autopsy?"

"Yep. Stomach contents was beef and hair. Veal, to be more exact. But, it's possible this one in back could be a wolf from Yellowstone. Park boundaries don't mean anything to wild animals."

Laura disagrees and in her authoritative tone begins to expound, "Almost all the Yellowstone wolves wear transmitter collars. And Fish and Game says none of theirs are anywhere near here."

Duane turns towards her in disbelief.

"I called!" she announces proudly with a sly grin.

He turns his head slowly and looks at her with bewilderment.

After a couple of seconds, Laura looks back and grins again. "Wanna hear my how-far-wolves-can-travel speech again?"

Duane smiles back, relaxes.

They continue bouncing up hill to Los Lobos Cabin with the body bag dancing sadly in the truck bed.

63

Den of Wolves

In cloud-muted moonlight, a pack of wolves runs through a pasture, leaping and yipping with delight. They twist and kiss one another in a obvious spurt of glee.

They stop, drink from a small stream then continue to race around and play. Suddenly, Kusko stops playing.

The others stop and instantly follow their Alpha male and begin to slowly circle a group of sheep lying in the pasture nearby. Hearing the earlier commotion, some of the sheep have sprung to their feet and begun to scatter.

The wolves single out several very young lambs still lying on the grass. Within seconds a lone wolf has accomplished the goal and the smallest and weakest lamb has drawn its last breath. After the kill, the pack has a victory howl that echoes through the pastures along River Road.

Later, as direct moonlight streams in from a crevice in the large boulders on either side of their den, the adult wolves sleep as one large mound of fur. Two pups whimper and squirm a bit, then fall asleep next to and all over the Alpha male.

A dead lamb's bloody head rests in the dirt next to the entrance. One lone pup gnaws at it half-heartedly.

Soon all the residents of the den are asleep. Soft snoring and grunting are contained within its walls of stone.

64

Your Lyin' Ways

Laura, Duane and Keith sit in a booth in the darkened, closed cafe. Crystal joins them, carrying four cups of coffee on a small tray. She is eager for news. One dim overhead light shines on their table.

Laura, bursting with ideas and comments, begins the conversation, "I still don't believe a thing Gregg has said about either the dead wolf or the letter. He was lyin' for sure, but why I don't know."

Crystal stares in admiration at Laura who continues her rapid-fire analysis.

"You could see he was obviously upset when he saw the dead wolf. Looked for a split second like he'd lost his kid or something. No doubt she's theirs, though he tried to act nonchalant. Remember, I had seen Tundra before, too, and believe it was definitely her."

Duane tries in vain to get a word in edgewise.

Laura plows on, "Brian could identify her for sure. We should email him a photo."

Duane takes another breath and opens his mouth to speak, but Laura fills the space again. "I also didn't buy Gregg's story that their wolves wouldn't even know how to kill a calf."

When Laura pauses for a breath, Keith takes the floor, "Right, that's bullshit! It's a wild animal. Killin's pure instinct. Ya shoulda seen that wolf that come up to Larry's truck."

He seems to relish his new status with the group. All three are
listening and watching him recount the incident.

"We was scared, for sure. She looked like she coulda ate us for
dinner. I ain't kiddin' neither."

Again Duane starts to comment but is cut off by Laura who
doesn't respond to Keith's observations and continues rambling,
"Maybe Gregg didn't admit it 'cuz he thinks it's a bad precedent to
pay Johnson for the dead calves! That would be admitting that they
were actually his."

For the third time, Duane loses his chance to answer. His cell
phone goes off, he checks it and immediately heads for the patrol car.

It's heard peeling out, lights flashing and siren on.

65

Snowball's Hell

Across the river in the moonlight, a large coyote slinks past a corral near the barn to the small ranch house where an overweight and fluffy white cat sleeps on a cushioned wooden chair. Cat toys are scattered around the screened-in porch with its door ajar.

Inside, a man and woman talk in low tones. She's knitting; he's polishing a leather saddle on a padded saw-horse-type frame.

A distinct sound, that of a wooden chair falling over onto the porch's cement floor and the piercing screech of an animal's last and desperate outcry, startles the couple.

They both drop what they're holding and leap to their feet. The woman runs onto the porch and flips on the overhead light. At her feet lies a bloody patch of once-white fur. In the distance she sees what she thinks is a silhouetted wolf slinking into the woods with the cat hanging limply from its mouth.

"Oh, God, Bill! One of those wolves just got Snowball!" she screams as she watches in horror, holding her hands over her mouth and sobbing.

Her husband, crying himself, pulls her close and stares off into the trees

66

Cat Fight

In his patrol car, Duane drives rapidly back down River Road toward Big Timber as he punches in a number on his cell phone. After a few seconds, Laura answers.

"Hi. Sorry I had to beat it out of there. Wild night."

In her nightgown, Laura lies atop her rumpled bed. When she hears Duane's voice, she smiles and snuggles down under the covers, talks in a sexy voice, "It has been quite a few hours. You poor thing. Wanna tell me your troubles?"

"Two more reports about more dead calves, a couple lambs and possibly the Anderson's cat!"

Laura bolts up in bed, "Oh, no! All killed by wolves?"

"Yep. Kathy Anderson said she's positive it was a wolf she saw with Snowball, her cat, in its mouth," Duane says. "Really freaked her out! I'm leaving their place now and heading home."

"Pretty awful night up here in the Crazies,"she says with empathy.

Duane adds, "That's not all. Kids down at the lake with pot, raisin' hell. Stoned outta their minds. Almost pushed a tourist's car into the water from the boat-launch ramp."

Laura sounds sarcastic, "How inviting for our tourists! Lovely! People who haven't already cancelled their reservations will for sure do it now!"

"Yep!" Duane says.

"So, did you arrest the kids?"

"Of course! What else would I do?"

"Don't know. You didn't arrest Gregg and he was stoned and even growing the stuff!"

Duane sits forward, his eyes bulging as if he can't believe what he has just heard, one hand squeezing the steering wheel until his knuckles turn white. He blurts out, "Now you really are telling me how to do my job. Again! This crosses the line, Laura!"

Laura's mood shifts. She swings her legs over the bedside and stands. She sounds self-righteous, "I'm telling you, Duane, you're losin' it. You don't arrest Gregg because you feel sorry for him. You can relate to him because you're convinced that, like you, his wife left him. But, you don't feel sorry at all or relate to the pothead kids."

Laura shifting into her lecture tone, "My therapist, Dr. Marshall, even warned me about this happening. He said there is something called the cry-wolf syndrome and people who have it make up their minds illogically."

Duane's anger and voice rise together and he instantly cuts her off in mid-sentence. "Enough! Enough, Laura! Don't quote me crap about what a Texas therapist said to you. You are a crime victim; I am NOT! It doesn't apply to my work as an investigator. You know what? You 're becoming completely insufferable!"

Laura blinks at his outburst and characterization of her.

Duane sounds royally pissed off and adds, "Gotta go. Talk to you some other time. Or not."

He pushes the disconnect key, throws the cell phone down on the passenger's seat, and pounds his fist on the steering wheel.

Laura throws a pillow across the room.

Destiny ducks under the bed.

67

Wake-up Call

Laura, on her laptop, checks the clock next to the couch. It reads 2 a.m. when she picks up the phone and punches in a number. Her tone is serious.

"Duane? Sorry to wake you, but I think I've really got something."

Duane, phone in hand, rolls over, looks at the clock. He rubs his eyes and tries to focus.

"Laura? Uh, huh? What now?"

She sounds excited as she holds a sheet of paper.

"I emailed some of my old police buddies in Texas to run a nation-wide background check on Gregg.

"And?" Duane gives her his full attention with no hint of leftovers from their previous interaction.

"His first wife died in a weird accident and he was a suspect."

Duane sits straight up. He looks wide awake now.

"Where did this happen? When?"

"I'll forward you what they sent me," she says, somewhat out of breath. "My friend, who's now a lieutenant in the Fort Worth P.D., told me he thought Gregg was dirty."

"So, Ms. Reporter, you're saying Evie may very well be lying stiff among the coffee grounds?"

He pauses for a moment and then adds with sincerity, "Hate to admit it, but I may just have to apologize to you again."

"Could be," Laura says without glee. "We need to find Evie before it's too late, if it isn't already."

"Guess I'll be checking in with our boy again. I'll call Sheriff Fuller first thing in the morning after I get to the office and open your email. By the way, I never did tell him about Gregg digging in his front yard with the backhoe. Let's get some sleep now. I gotta get up in a few hours."

He doesn't wait for a response. He hangs up.

This time, though, Laura holds the phone a few seconds and feels calm about Duane, his reaction and his new belief in her judgment.

68

Feeding Frenzy

It's 3 a.m. and Keith, Tim and Larry lie on their stomachs in the bright moonlight on the hillside above Los Lobos Cabin. They all use binoculars.

Suddenly, Larry spots something and blurts out in a loud whisper, "Holy shit! Check this out! Over there by that wolf pen!"

The others strain to focus their binoculars.

Two wolves trot back into the compound from the parking area. Gregg, apparently hearing something, has come out to investigate, rifle in hand.

"Christ! He's goin' kill 'em!" Tim gasps with alarm.

Then, Gregg puts down his rifle, starts petting them and the wolves jump up, their paws resting on his shoulders. They lick his face. Their ears flatten and their tails hang low in submission.

Gregg pushes them off him, walks quickly back into the cabin, leaving his rifle on the ground. After several minutes, he returns with what looks like large chunks of meat.

The wolves cry out impatiently, jumping and competing. They nearly knock him down with their enthusiasm. He tosses the meat away from him and onto the ground. They rush to pick it up and in seconds, they dash back into the woods and out of sight.

"Where the hell they goin'?" Keith whispers.

They watch Gregg with his rifle hanging limply over his arm walking back to the cabin. He closes the door and the lights go out immediately.

The three men begin to ease backward down the hill. Larry stumbles and falls over a large object. He uses a flashlight to examine it closer. The light reveals a large bloody bone. The blood looks fresh. Pieces of what look to him like human flesh loosely hang from it.

The three stare at one another, speechless, then look back at the bone. Keith, appears disgusted but hesitantly reaches down, picks it up and takes it along as they make their way back to the truck.

69

Remaining Silent

It's mid-morning. Duane and Gregg sit at the spool table. Gregg looks sober but scruffy; he needs a bath, a shave. He hasn't changed clothes for days either. Duane notices and sits as close as possible to the open window. A video plays in the adjoining room. It shows somewhat recent footage of Evie with the wolves at Los Lobos Cabin. Duane sees one scene of the pack on their mattresses inside the cabin's wolf den.

She appears to be asleep surrounded by snoring wolves on the dirty wall-to-wall mattresses. Through the den window, big flakes of snow can be seen floating down outside. Evie looks innocent, natural.

"I wanted to build them a separate compound, an outside shelter. Evie said it would hurt their feelings not to be inside with us. Only time they sleep outside is when the females have pups."

"They even sleep inside in the summer, too?" Duane asks.

Gregg nods, looking especially sad.

The video switches to a segment showing Tundra's pups in the special area of the fenced wolf compound. The pups get total attention from the pack. The other wolves tend to them, licking and playing with them.

Then sounding more lucid than Duane has ever heard him before, Gregg states, "Wolves look on pups as communal babies.

They all care for them, groom them and even baby-sit them. They're the whole pack's responsibility. It's built in. That's why I just can't understand how Evie could do this to them."

Duane looks at Gregg and his tone changes to deadly serious.

"Mr. Ballard, I'd like to ask you a few questions, if you don't mind."

Duane removes a card from his shirt pocket and reads directly from it, not looking at Gregg, "You have the right to remain silent..."

As Duane finishes the sentences, suddenly Gregg clicks off the television and stares at him in disbelief.

"You're actually reading me my Miranda rights?"

"Yes, I just did," Duane says with professionalism. With no further comment, Duane begins the interrogation.

"Your first wife, I think her name was Helen?"

"Yeah. What about her?"

"Didn't she die in rather unusual circumstances?"

Gregg looks uncomfortable; he lights a cigarette.

Duane, stone-faced, uses a small note pad and a pen and begins to take notes.

"Yeah, I guess you'd say that. She died hiking in Arches National Park. Fell off the trail. Broke her neck. That was 15 years ago, for God's sakes! Before I ever went to Alaska to teach. What's that got to do with Evie being missing?"

"Wasn't there an investigation, charging you with her death?"

Gregg looks shocked. He stands, says nothing more and walks out of the room.

Clearly, the interview is over.

70

Just a Note

Laura is on the laptop. She's written a short email and is proofing it. As she reads, she's aware that she should be observing her own written warnings and backing off what could be a dangerous situation.

In a fleeting moment, she remembers Dr. Marshall's warning about people sometimes ignoring all logical explanations and drawing an opposite conclusion than obvious facts indicate.

She hesitates for a split second and instead of DELETE pushes SEND.

Jo:

I know what you're thinking. I shouldn't be involved with any possible murder investigation, and I shouldn't be involved with any sheriff's deputy either. Or any wolves for that matter. Too late on all counts. Color me involved. Later, Laura

71

Tenting Tonight

At sun-up, Laura, Jerry, several wranglers and a large group guests of all ages from Timberline Ranch mount their horses in the large corral next to the barn.

Three mules are packed with rolled-up tents, sleeping bags, air mattresses and cooking gear. Jerry leads the way. Laura is last in line on Solo while Destiny and two of the ranch dogs, bandanas around their necks, run alongside the group, stopping to sniff and investigate.

Other ranch staff members wave a send-off. It's the only overnight trail ride of the year and many guests have reserved their places six months to a year in advance. Some families return year after year for the special cookout-campout.

The line of 15 horses plus mules winds its way slowly up the trail through a pasture next to a rapidly running stream. Spectacular views surround them.

Above timberline they pass a large cave close to, but somewhat above, the trail. Some of the younger guests point it out to Laura.

Others try to take photos while bobbing along on their horses.

She acknowledges their requests to check out the cave entrance as she passes by it. For a few seconds, she has an eerie feeling about it, and then that quickly passes. She then concentrates on her trail duties, making sure that children maintain control of their horses, that horses are not allowed to stop and eat, and generally keeping things moving forward.

The group arrives at the camp site which has both a horse corral and a separate, very large cooking area with a fire pit.

With the help of the wranglers, the group dismounts, removes the saddles and saddle blankets and places them and the bridles on the split-rail fences around the corral.

Horses are released into the corral. Some of the horses and two of the mules lie down and roll in the dust as if to erase the memories of the heavy loads on their backs.

Laura, Jerry and the man everyone calls Cook, a Wilford Brimley lookalike, begin to set up camp and start meal preparations. Charlie, one of the wranglers, takes a bag of feed and pours it into the horse troughs, while Steve fills the horses' water troughs, taking bucket after bucket from the stream.

Dudes help one another set up tents and organize their gear. Several yards away from the corral, an old outhouse with its door hanging precariously on one hinge is repaired by Eddie who also places some fresh rolls of toilet paper inside.

With all the activity, the area resembles an old western town during the gold rush era but without covered wagons. Nothing modern is in evidence. The dudes are loving it, taking photos right and left.

After a few hours, everyone pitches in to help serve the barbecue dinner with steaks, beans and corn, topped off by pineapple upside-down cakes baked over the fire in Dutch ovens. For more than an hour, people eat with abandon, commenting how especially good everything tastes in the outdoors.

Wine for the adults flows freely before and during dinner, while cowboy coffee in an oversized pot steeps on the edge of the campfire.

Eddie, Charlie, Jerry and Laura help clear the dishes taking directions from Cook as the guests gather around the fireside for the music and singing.

Suddenly Laura comes running toward Cook and Jerry who have finished their chores and are sitting on the ground around the campfire with the dudes.

Steve is playing a guitar and singing as everyone chimes in on the chorus of "Home on the Range."

Youngsters toast marshmallows over the campfire's embers.

Laura urgently signals Jerry and Cook and they quickly slip away from the circle to talk with her in hushed tones behind some trees.

"We got big problems!" Laura whispers. "I went to put away the rest of the cream for the coffee, and the coolers with all of tomorrow's food inside have been broken into!"

Alarmed, the men follow her back to a clearing. They see two coolers damaged and overturned, broken egg shells everywhere and food containers empty and dirty. A torn canvas pack lays in the dirt.

Jerry's hand covers his mouth. He shakes his head in disbelief. "Damn! Think it was a bear? Anything left?"

Cook searches around frantically reporting immediately, "Only the bread and some jam I had in another pack. What the fuck am I supposed to feed the dudes tomorrow mornin'?"

"This is a disaster!" Jerry chokes out. "Nothin' like this ever happened before, not in the ten years we've been doin' this!"

Laura examines the coolers and the torn pack and notices the prints next to them. Animal prints are everywhere.

"Check this out!" she exclaims.

Cook and Jerry investigate, see the tracks and look stunned.

"Holy crap! No doubt what them hippies' wolves had fer supper!"

Cook takes off his cowboy hat, scratches his head and says with disgust, "Seven pounds bacon, six pounds sausage, six dozen eggs and four pounds of cheese. They did all right!"

Then after a short discussion with the two men, Laura begins to saddle Solo. Jerry gives her a torch-style flashlight. Cook hands her a plastic water bottle. She loops the flashlight strap over the saddle horn and places the water bottle into her saddle bag. She mounts Solo and talks quietly to Jerry.

"Down in the Valley" is being sung in the background.

"I should be back before anybody gets up in the morning."

"Sure you don't want me to go? It don't feel right you bein' all by yourself."

"No. You two guys need to be here for the dudes. I can do this."

Destiny, tail wagging, looks up at Laura on Solo and seems to realize she's going for a walk.

"Destiny will be good company. Besides, Solo can walk that trail blindfolded."

"It's a good thing, too," Jerry says. "Fog's comin' in. Big time!"

Laura looks up as the moon is becoming obscured by low clouds.

"I just hope Vince can get them to open the general store. No place else in Big Timber has that much extra grub this late at night," Cook says.

"We won't mention this to the dudes unless you don't get back by sunrise. For all they know, we do it this way ever' time just to be sure we have fresh food," Jerry says, forcing a smile. "Be careful, Laura!" he adds with concern. "Got the mobile phone?"

"Right here," Laura answers, patting her jacket pocket.

"As you get close to the ranch, give Vince a call. He can get Keith up to speed with the food order," Jerry says. "If he's not there, have him get Crystal to give us everything she can from the cafe.

"Vince is gonna croak! If this news gets out, there won't be an east-coast dude anywhere near the state of Montana!" Laura says, shaking her head.

Cook looks worried about her comment, "Jerry, you and me better stay up all night watching them dudes' tents. Wouldn't be good if them wolves was to come back."

Jerry, grim-faced, nods in agreement.

Laura kicks Solo's sides gently to start him back down the trail.

72

Flight of Fantasy

Gregg sits with only a single lamp on, drinking beer and smoking a joint. The short reefer burns close to his fingers, its smoke swirling. He stands at the cabin door and stares out in a stupor. What he thinks he sees is blurred and dreamlike. He blinks his eyes and tries to focus.

A hazy figure, a woman in a flowered skirt, appears to him through the fog. She walks in slow motion up near the compound. She waves to him and smiles. He begins to talk to her in slurred speech.

"Shit, Evie, why couldn't you just let things alone? Why was it always the wolves, yours and Brian's wolves, the wolves, always them and never me?"

As he staggers outside, he turns on the porch light, muttering, "Ya wore out the God-damned video staring at fuckin' Brian, day after day after day."

The bright porch light illuminates the yellow backhoe near the wolf compound. Off-and-on fog obscures the moon.

The excavation site has been compacted and smoothed somewhat. With no human or animal in sight, he walks down the stairs and stumbles to the backhoe, gets on, fires it up and begins to dig.

After a few bucketsful, a large piece of Evie's dirty flowered skirt is unearthed.

He immediately stops the backhoe, gets off and falters back toward the cabin, his hands over his face. The remnants of Evie's skirt hang from the back-hoe's bucket.

Gregg turns away and cries out into the night, "Evie forgive me! Please forgive me!"

Unable to walk, he falls to the ground, his face in the dirt, and mumbles, "God, help me!"

He passes out in his tracks.

73

Crystal Clear

Duane, Keith and Crystal sip coffee in the back booth. Three truckers hold up their cups after finishing their meal to signal Crystal for refills. She gets up, picks up the coffee pot, pours some for the truckers and comes back, filling up their own cups before sitting back down to hear the latest news from Duane.

"So, Crabtree's also lost a couple lambs, Sambar's a couple calves?" Crystal asks Duane.

"Coulda been bears, don't ya think?" Keith asks Duane before he can answer.

"A bear'll usually kill one animal. Only a wolf pack would do this much damage. Remember, there are eleven or more of them to feed."

"Wolf man's bills keep goin' up and up," Crystal adds.

"Sambar was in this afternoon. Said they found one carcass. Nothin' much left. Just a trail of blood into the woods," Keith says.

The three continue to sip coffee.

74

Night Light

Laura shines the flashlight over Solo's head as they slowly make their way back down the trail.

"We're half way there. Doin' good, Solo."

She pats his neck and realizes she and Solo are a team. To her, with his actions, he epitomizes loyalty, strength and security. He is like a silent, always-there friend she can rely on without having to specifically ask him for help. Instinctively, he knows what she needs.

As he steadily and surely walks on, she recalls a quote from Shakespeare's *Richard III*, "A horse, a horse, my kingdom for a horse!" and understands fully tonight, that quite literally she alone cannot complete this important job without Solo. Nothing, absolutely nothing and no-one else will do.

They cross a stream. Destiny splashes ahead. Suddenly, Laura's flashlight seems to dim. She shakes it roughly. It brightens momentarily, then quits altogether.

Blackness is everywhere. Thick fog rolls in.

"Damn it! I can't believe this!" she cries out.

She shakes the flashlight again. Nothing. Solo stumbles on a rock. He catches himself and recovers, plodding on. Destiny follows Laura's commands as she calls out, "Here, girl. Here, Destiny."

75

Cries in the Night

Fog continues to shroud the trail as Destiny suddenly races ahead. Wolves begin to howl in harmony close by the cave Laura and the dudes saw earlier.

Destiny runs toward the howling. Then, a bone-chilling wail, almost like a human voice, is heard. Startled, Laura strains to see. Solo shies suddenly.

"Ohhhhhhhhhh," echoes through the canyons.

Laura is stunned. She leans forward in the saddle. Destiny barks. Then total silence.

Destiny cocks her head, whines and listens. Nothing.

Laura looks as if she doubts her own ears. She feels certain she has just heard a human voice. She pulls out the mobile phone. Her tone is urgent.

"Jerry, come in."

"I'm here, Laura."

"Bad news. Flashlight went dead. I'm down near the cave."

"Shit! What next? You stay put. I'll be right there. Got another flashlight I'll bring you."

"No need. Solo's doing okay. Fog is spotty. I'll let you know if we go zero-zero."

Destiny continues to bark at the darkness near the cave.

"What's with Destiny?" he asks, hearing her barking.

"Think maybe she may have found some of the missing wolves."

"Want me to try to get a hold of Duane? Or maybe you could raise Vince and have him call Duane?"

"Not much he could do tonight. But something else weird happened."

"What?"

"Thought I heard weird sounds coming from the cave."

"What kind of weird sounds?"

"Wolves and…" her voice fades out.

"Laura? You okay?"

Just then Solo stumbles again in the darkness but he quickly recovers.

She doesn't finish her thought, "Probably nothing. Just my imagination working over-time. If it wasn't so damned foggy again, I could probably see the ranch lights from here."

"Can't hear you too good, Laura, you're fadin' out."

"Not too far now. We're almost back below timberline. Jerry? Jerry?"

Silence.

"Shit!" Laura mutters, putting the mobile phone back into her jacket pocket.

Solo's clip-clopping makes the only sounds as they pass the cave. Several pairs of unseen amber eyes peer out as the moon breaks through the fog. Sensing something, Destiny perks up her ears and begins to backtrack toward the cave. Laura calls her, nudges Solo softly with her heels, and the trio continues down the trail.

When Laura arrives at the graveyard, she nudges Solo again to move forward but she mentally retreats.

"Would you identify for the court the person you found in the locked metal tool box? Is that person present in court?"

"Yes. She's sitting in the front row with the blue dress on," the officer says pointing to Laura.

The members of the jury and everyone in the court stare at her as she looks up and locks eyes with the officer.

*"Let the record show the witness has identified Laura Black,"
the prosecutor says as the court reporter's machine clicks in
response.*

*Sitting facing the judge, a man wearing an orange jail jumpsuit
with chains around his waist attached to his handcuffs, has his
back to her. He slowly turns around and stares at Laura with an
almost imperceptible grin. Startled, she shudders and looks away.
Those in the courtroom witnessing his expression and her reaction
appear shocked.*

A gasp is heard from one side of the room.

Solo's trotting through the darkened area brings Laura back to
the present. She looks straight ahead, grips the saddle horn with both
hands to steady her nerves when she suddenly feels a panic attack
coming on and begins to whisper, prayer-like, "This is about Evie,
finding Evie. Do what you're afraid to do."

Suddenly, the lights of Timberline Ranch come into view.

76

Come 'n Get It!

Cook serves food to the hungry and appreciative campers in the chow-line. Jerry and Laura look on, smiling with satisfaction as the wranglers next to her drink coffee.

"Did your breakfast taste real good, Laura?" Cook asks as if in code. "Had to feed the crew first to be sure."

"Wonderful!" she answers, smiling. "Really fresh food!"

"Only the best for our dudes!" Cook adds, winking back.

"Wasn't really a big deal," Laura says. "Vince easily located Keith and he headed up to the ranch with the stuff immediately."

Jerry smirks. "Keith ain't hard to find. Stays pretty close to his videos."

She grins slightly, "They even got the saddlebags packed really fast. It was a quick ride back up here and Vince rode up with me on Tango and then rode Solo back down. He didn't want me coming back up here alone in the middle of the night."

Jerry yawns. Laura joins him.

They both sigh as they watch people devour the food.

77

Up In the Air

A helicopter flies low over the area between the ranch and Los Lobos Cabin.

Pilot Skip Hay, in jeans and a western shirt, quietly concentrates, his eyes on the mountain pass ahead.

Duane sits beside him, scanning the landscape as Skip expertly negotiates the chopper through the narrow pass, flying just above the trees and rock formations. Light turbulence lifts the craft and then drops it as wind gusts circulate near the pass entrance.

Laura sits in back.

"Thanks for doing this, Skip. Don't see anything here. Noise probably spooked 'em. How about farther down the canyon?" Duane says into his headset microphone.

"Roger that, Duane," Skip responds, deftly turning the craft 180 degrees.

"Ranchers' sheep were killed a ways down river," Duane says.

Laura, who is without a microphone or headset, urgently taps Skip on the shoulder, shouts over the noise of the engine and points to a specific rock formation below near the trail, saying, "Circle right over there!"

He nods and turns the craft back to the left and the three continue to scan the area as the helicopter hovers then closes in on the outcropping Laura has pointed out.

Suddenly, over one formation, Duane spots something below.

"Wolf!" Duane shouts. "Right down there!"

The animal has briefly looked up and appears to bark, then races away, disappearing behind the formation. Skip continues to fly tight circles, but there seems to be no further movement.

"Bet the others are around there somewhere," Skip says.

"Let's set down here and take a look," Duane suggests.

"Not a chance! Way too rocky!" Skip says. "Starting to get dark, too."

The narrow canyon is surrounded by twisted shrubs, huge boulders and loose rocks,.

What local hikers experience, but trail riders miss, Duane and Laura seem captivated by as they stare in wonder while Skip makes one last scan of the area. Over centuries, a smooth glacial slide pushed through to create a pathway for a waterfall.

Skip watches their faces as he shows them a pilot's perspective.

Just below timberline, a few aspen struggle where sunlight hits the highest crags, bringing life forth from stone. Orange and green algae and lichen cling to the steep canyon walls where two big-horn sheep seem to hang in mid-air as they forage for sparse grasses tucked in crevices.

It is clear that there is no level place to land safely.

The chopper turns to leave, crossing back over the loop trail toward Timberline Ranch.

"Well, we know where to head first thing in the morning," Duane says to Skip.

78

Shedding Some Light

Dawn seems to have come too soon for Laura, Jerry and wranglers Bob and Steve as they finish saddling up and start out of the corral on their way back up to the overnight campsite. The men have rifles stowed on their saddles. Vince has asked them to ensure the wolves are not permanently holed up anywhere on ranch property. His point is well-taken. Kill them before they kill again.

They pass Destiny who is firmly tied to the corral fence. A full water bowl sits within her reach. She seems desperate to follow them and begins to chew at her leather leash. Nobody notices.

As the foursome slowly exits the area, Jerry commiserates with Bob and Steve who smoke, yawn and complain about getting up before dawn.

"Didn't we just get back from up there, hauling all the crap from the campout? Now here we go again," Steve grumbles.

Laura sighs and nods back.

"Duane may join us later, but he just had a call about somebody's German Shepherd being killed," Laura says. "Dog was owned by a big contributor to Sheriff Fuller's election campaign, so he couldn't just ignore it."

"Musta been the McGrath's. They're loaded. Have a couple shepherds, too," Jerry adds.

Without additional conversation, the others follow Jerry single file and begin to make their way back up the trail. They seem somewhat anxious, not sure about what awaits them.

Just before they arrive at the rock outcropping where the wolf was spotted from the helicopter, Laura overtakes Jerry and signals for the group to stop. She holds her finger to her lips for everyone to be quiet.

As they dismount, she whispers, "Let's tie the horses down here away from the cave."

"Yep. Wolves might spook 'em," Jerry agrees.

"Wolves freak me out, too," Steve says with a worried look on his face.

79

Full Circle

Gregg slumps in front of his television set, watching a newscaster show an enlarged Google map of the area around Los Lobos Cabin.

A bright red circle has been drawn directly over the Los Lobos Cabin wolf compound. Gregg holds his hand over his mouth and feels an overwhelming sense of sadness sweep over him.

"And this is where we believe at least eleven wolves escaped."

Another map appears with several distinct black circles drawn around separate areas.

The newscaster uses an electronic pointer as he speaks,

"Here are locations where livestock and domestic pets have been killed in the past few days."

He points to more areas as circles are drawn electronically over nearby ranch lands.

The newscaster ends with, "And now back to the studio where news anchor Dorothy Maloney has a guest who will hopefully shed some more light on the wolf situation."

The program returns to the news desk where an attractive woman in her 40s looks into the camera, "Thank you, Bob."

"Now, I'd like to welcome Lynda Koehler, a wolf expert who has led the movement to reintroduce wolves into Yellowstone National Park for the past decade."

The camera focuses very close up on a well-dressed and nicely coiffed woman who appears to be very comfortable in front of the television camera. She smiles and nods when introduced.

"Ms. Koehler has just arrived from West Yellowstone where her foundation is located."

As he sees her on the screen, Gregg's eyes narrow and he becomes spitting mad. He throws his half-full beer bottle at the screen, splashing the liquid on it. It seems to run down the woman's face as she speaks. Beer drips onto the floor as the bottle rolls back toward the wall, leaving a wet trail.

Gregg folds his arms across his chest and scowls.

"Thank you for joining us, Lynda. Could you assure our viewers that the missing wolves are not a danger to the public?"

While her soft voice is heard in the background, a video plays on the screen. It shows a harmless-looking wolf chasing a rabbit through the Alaskan tundra. Koehler sounds like a professor and is reassuring as she explains wolf behavior.

"Their diet in the wild can consist mostly of large animals such as bison or deer, but they also hunt medium to small animals and rodents. They are known for killing weak, old or injured animals."

Her voiceover continues while the next video clip shows wolves taking down an obviously injured fawn. The program returns to the news desk.

"And do they ever attack or kill people?" Maloney asks, looking at Koehler.

"That is almost unheard of," Koehler answers, firmly. "Most experts think it's pure myth. Once these fictional stories about the big bad wolf, werewolves and so forth are repeated and passed down through the generations, starting in the Middle Ages, they spiral out of control and, unfortunately, people sometimes believe them as fact."

She shakes her head in dismay, adding, "A person has a much greater chance of being killed by a mountain lion or a bear. Or struck by lightning."

In disgust, Gregg stands, turns off the set and kicks the beer bottle, sending it spinning into the corner.

80

Into Thin Air

Steve, Jerry and Bob remove rifles from their saddle ties and load them. Each man has a hunting vest with additional ammunition, a bottle of water, matches and cigarettes.

They begin to hike slowly toward the cave area. Jerry turns off his mobile phone. No one is smiling. They all spot the cave entrance about the same time.

The altitude starts to take its toll. Everyone stops to catch their breath now that they, not their horses, are doing the climbing. Jerry and Bob open their water bottles and take long swigs.

"Wish this was a beer!" Jerry whispers without a smile.

Suddenly a blur of yellow fur streaks by.

Destiny dashes past them at a full run. She doesn't acknowledge or seem to see Laura or Jerry. Clearly, she's on a mission. She races to a point just beyond the cave, not into its entrance. She turns into the woods and begins to urgently sniff plants and undergrowth on both sides of her, then disappears.

Laura, stunned at Destiny's appearance on the scene, has no time to comment, and immediately realizes that the dog must either be wary of the wolf scent or may have seen or smelled something in the woods just beyond. She chooses not to call to Destiny fearing she might frighten whatever lies ahead or is inside the cave.

Jerry says nothing either and begins to inch toward the cave. He signals to the others to remain quiet. They all tiptoe forward, rifles pointed down. He carries a flashlight and his rifle in a somewhat awkward and uncoordinated manner, trying to balance and turn on the light in the process.

Just as his flashlight starts to illuminate the dark entrance to the cave, a large wolf bolts from inside. Startled, Jerry jumps back, knocks down Steve and the two of them fall into a heap. One of the rifles discharges.

Bob spins around and shakily aims at the escaping wolf. He fires. The wolf is gone.

Laura gasps, panicked about Destiny's location.

Jerry and Steve again move toward the cave's opening. Destiny is still nowhere to be seen.

Laura proceeds forward, shaken. She slowly walks inside and allows her eyes to adjust. Then, she shines her own flashlight toward a back wall, and motions for the others to join her. She discovers shallow holes with pieces of dirt-covered bacon and sausage, some still wrapped in plastic.

Using his boot, Steve kicks dirt from some of the pieces. "Breakfast anyone?" he whispers sarcastically. The men explore adjoining areas of the cave.

Laura slowly walks alone toward the back. She bends down slightly to avoid hitting her head. She suddenly stops, squats down with her flashlight and visually inspects an imprint on the cave floor. She recognizes a partial print in the dust. It is definitely that of a bare-footed human. She says nothing to the others. Another print is about six inches away. Again, she says nothing, almost as if it hasn't registered as significant.

All around the cave floor are scores of distinct wolf prints of various sizes.

She uses her flashlight to broadly illuminate them. The three men stand still. They have definitely seen the wolf prints, too, and realize without any conversation that they don't know if the wolves are inside or outside the cave. Each man slowly backs out.

Hearing them exit, Destiny dashes from the trees, eager to reunite at the cave's entrance. She remains quiet, only her tail wagging, when she sees Laura. The foursome ignores her and soon she slowly trots behind the group as they make their way back to their horses and ultimately to Timberline Ranch.

Hours later the men are back at the ranch bar, drinking heavily and discussing how to break the news to Vince that they've returned empty-handed.

81

Crazy Arms

Laura and Duane drive with all the windows open. She seems comfortable riding in the closed-in car. She's deeply breathing in fresh air and doesn't appear to be stressed at all. Duane notices but says nothing.

The day is spectacular. A cloudless blue sky frames the far mountains. On a rustic bridge, they pass over a crystal-clear creek cascading through the woods.

Against regulations, Duane has old-time western love songs playing on a portable CD player plugged into the cigarette lighter. He has forgotten to toss his latest romance novel into the back seat. It sits in the cup holder clearly visible.

Laura sees it and picks it up as if it's contagious, holding it with two fingers and acting as if it's giving off a bad odor.

"Who's been in the patrol car and left this?"

Sheepishly, Duane raises his hand, "Guilty, as charged. Now you know my secret."

"You can't be serious!" Laura declares. "God, how can you stand these things?" she asks with disdain.

"Easy," he replies, as Laura continues to shake her head in disbelief.

"I like a happy ending," he adds without apology. "And there's not always one in real life."

Laura pitches the paperback onto the back seat.

"Tell me about it!" she mumbles, not looking at Duane.

They proceed without further comment, listening to the western music.

"You and the guys got so close to finding the wolves and then, nothing. Even almost shot one. You saw where they'd been. We've gotta find where they are now. This is a disaster for the dude ranches. This is the peak of the tourist season!"

She reaches over and angrily turns down the music.

"Right. And what about Evie? When will it be *her* season?"

Duane reaches over and turns up the music, this time increasing its volume. He looks exasperated and can barely spit out his words.

"Ya know, Laura. I'm dropping you off at your place. You're really interfering with my work. I shouldn't even have you with me, since you're not officially in the media or helping with the investigation."

His words sting.

She slips down into the seat and looks sullen.

"And your so-called investigation has to do with dead calves, lambs and campaign contributors' pets? Not people, I assume?" she stabs back at him.

She waits a few seconds before adding, "You realize you've just given up on Evie!"

Duane ignores her, his eyes staring straight ahead.

Thinking of Evie lying in the hole in front of Los Lobos Cabin, Laura closes her eyes.

The tool box is opened. One police officer shines a light inside. The other pulls Laura out. She can hear an old woman's voice nearby. She seems to be coming closer to speak to Laura.

She has a thick Texas accent, "Police, ever'body, said I was nuts, but I just wouldn't give up on ya, darlin'," she says directly to Laura who can hear but not see her, her eyes not yet adjusting to the glare.

"I called the cops three times 'fore they come out here. I just knew somethin' wasn't right when I saw them men puttin' that big

metal box in that old mausoleum. Hadn't been nobody buried there for years. Besides, they didn't look sad at all, seemed more like they was gettin' rid of something they didn't want no more."

Laura's eyes open suddenly. She sits straight up. Duane flashes her a drop-dead look. Arms folded across her chest, she continues to stare at him with contempt.

When the old Ray Price classic, "*Crazy Arms*" comes on the CD, and she hears the words," *Crazy arms that long to hold somebody new..."* her jaws become set.

"Crazy in the Crazies!" she mutters to herself.

When the patrol car rolls to a stop in front of her cabin, Laura gets out, slams the door and stomps toward her front door without looking back.

Duane sits staring straight ahead for a few seconds, his hands gripping the steering wheel. He angrily ejects the CD.

Destiny peers out of the cabin's front window as Laura approaches.

After a few seconds, the patrol car drives away.

82

New Old News

Uncharacteristically, Keith is watching CNN with the volume up in the back room of the general store with the curtain open when Duane enters, walks to the coffee pot and pours himself a cup.

Keith emerges and seems eager to talk."Hey, Duane. Anything new?"

"Nothin' worth discussing," Duane grumbles.

Suddenly, Keith takes on an air of importance, "Ya know, we're big in the news now. Me and the guys been on ever' channel, plus CNN. Even got a call from Alaska, too. They asked me stuff about the wolves and them hippies. Been real interestin'."

He grins broadly, obviously delighted by the publicity and his new-found celebrity.

Duane is not amused.

"Shit, Keith, this is a public-relations disaster for the dude ranches up here! Most of 'em have had 80 percent cancellations this week. And what they don't need is you on an ego trip at their expense! Get it?" he scowls.

Keith tries to tone down his enthusiasm, tries to look concerned. A few seconds pass and he attempts to make up.

"Anything new about the wolf man's wife?"

Duane, sighs, calms down and leans up next to the counter to sip his coffee.

"Nothin' at all. Saw her friend, that wolf expert, on television. Gonna call the station to try to get her number and see if she's heard from Evie."

Keith takes a deep breath and looks contrite. He doesn't have eye contact with Duane.

Still hesitating, Keith painfully spits out a few words, "Guess I shoulda told ya this before."

Duane sips his coffee, waiting but not expecting too much, then he walks over to grab a candy bar.

Keith continues, "But, after some beers, me and the guys went up to them hippies' cabin real late the other night to, er, check things out."

Duane can't believe his ears, "You what?"

We climbed up the hill above their place and saw 'ol Gregg feedin' two wolves by hand."

Duane is furious. He slams the cup down on the counter spilling most of his coffee and stares in disbelief at him.

"Christ, Keith! Why didn't you call me with this information? Might have saved some time and effort if we'd known where to track them. We've had people all over hell and gone."

"There was just them two wolves. Didn't tell ya 'cuz I thought you'd be pissed at us for bein' up there. Sorry."

Duane turns and heads for the door. He throws the candy back toward Keith who dodges it.

Duane slows his pace when, out of the corner of his eye, he sees Keith reach under the counter and bring out a large black plastic bag and start to follow him.

"One more thing," Keith says with his renewed sense of importance, but sounding as if he's also trying to get back on Duane's good side.

Out of curiosity, Duane stops and turns around. Keith opens the bag and pulls out the large bloody bone.

83

Begging the Question

Frantic, Laura shakes some kibbles from a box into Destiny's bowl while putting on lipstick with her other hand. Her cell phone rings. Dropping the lipstick onto the kitchen counter where it leaves a blob of red goo, she races to locate her phone and finds it inside her purse which is sitting under piles of junk on the couch. She clicks it on and balances it between her ear and shoulder.

"Black," she states officiously in her reporter's voice she thought she left behind in the newsroom. She listens to determine who's on the other end and quickly recognizes the caller.

"Hi. Yeah, I know. Shouldn't have gotten involved. Thanks for nothing, Jo, but, I have to see this through! Gotta go. I'll email you later. Promise. Gotta leave the cabin right now. Bye."

She pulls on one of her riding boots. She loses her balance, drops the other one onto the coffee table glass, not breaking it but startling Destiny who momentarily stops gobbling her food.

Laura hangs up, pulls on her other boot, grabs her car keys and opens the front door. Destiny leads the way down the stairs and waits for the passenger door to open. The outside of the convertible is filthy and the inside is full of junk. She takes some of it from the passenger seat and tosses it onto the floor of the backseat, leaving room for Destiny who quickly hops in to ride shotgun as usual.

Fearing she might lose some of the loose papers, Laura makes a practical decision to keep the top up and the wind out. She jumps in, starts the engine and oblivious to the seatbelt warning beeping continuously, drives to Timberline Ranch.

When she pulls into the parking lot, she sees three sheriffs' patrol cars parked near the dining hall. Several other cars, including a Montana Fish and Game pickup and a media van with a satellite dish raised for live transmitting, are parked near the entrance. The white van's sides and back doors are painted with, "Eyewitness News, Channel 7" in bright blue.

She parks and quickly walks with Destiny past the swimming pool and deck area which are deserted as is the horseshoe-throwing pit. A yellow plastic duck floats alone in the empty wading pool.

Ranch guests are nowhere to be seen.

When she enters the crowded dining hall, the meeting is already underway.

Duane sits at one of the main tables with two other deputies and Sheriff Jack Fuller. They face a full complement of ranchers, Timberline staff members and media types, using reporters' notebooks, cameras and microphones. Everyone is listening intently. Bright lights, television cameras and all eyes are focused on Fuller.

Laura takes a seat in the back row with Destiny lying at her feet.

Fuller speaks with authority, looking tense.

He is in mid-sentence,"...our plan is to use aircraft, mounted patrols and volunteers to scour the area until we find the remaining wolves."

A reporter interrupts him with another question, "Sheriff? Charlie Whale, CNN. You said you might have to destroy the wolves. Does that also include the wolf pups who might not be an actual threat to livestock?"

Before Fuller can respond, Laura smirks to herself as she immediately recognizes the reporter's interviewing technique of disguising one's already established opinion by framing it into a question. Journalists refer to it as a "have-you-stopped-beating-your-wife?" question. No matter how it is answered, it sounds bad.

"We'll take appropriate action to save any wolves we can," a somewhat rattled Fuller says, trying to put an end to that line of questioning.

Before that can happen, a no-nonsense blonde in tight jeans and an expensive beaded jean jacket jumps to her feet, holding a reporter's notebook and pen, "Lois Neil, CBS in Bozeman. Sheriff, how can you be sure you'll only shoot Arctic wolves, the ones missing from Los Lobos Cabin?"

Again Fuller, under pressure, tries to put his best spin on a bad situation, "Frankly, we haven't seen any gray wolves up here for more than a year. Shouldn't be a problem."

Laura begins to frantically wave her hand to get Fuller's attention. Duane frowns at her. She doesn't wait for Fuller to call on her. She stands and without any sense of embarrassment yells, "Sheriff? Back here!"

The cameraman turns around as does the sound man with a boom microphone who rushes back to her. Lights, camera and sound are now on her. Knowing she wants her question to end up on television, she waits for a couple of seconds as the entire crowd turns around, too.

Clearly and without a hint of intimidation, she identifies herself, "Laura Black, freelance writer. Sheriff Fuller, with all due respect, some people say since you're running for re-election in the fall that you've decided to do whatever it takes to end this public-relations nightmare."

Laura has made a comment; she has not asked a question and Fuller looks flustered. Fuller inhales and tries not to appear angry, but his tone borders on frustration.

"This has nothing to do with either PR or the election. Just doin' my job. I assume you aren't from around here, but those of us who are consider wolves killing livestock and possibly ruining our dude-ranch businesses to be bad for our area anytime, elections or not. I'll do whatever it takes to get us back to normal up here."

A few people in the crowd politely applaud. It isn't clear if they are clapping for Laura having courage to ask the tough question or for Fuller's response to it.

Duane locks eyes with Laura, stares daggers at her, and then leans over to the deputy closest to him, covers his microphone and softly mumbles, "Fuckin' reporters!"

The deputy smirks in reply.

Fuller takes a few more questions and regains his composure. The meeting is winding down. The sheriff thanks people and the press for coming, prepares to leave the front of the room, picks up some papers from the table, and begins to walk toward the back to exit the building. He starts to pass Laura.

The cameras and lights go off and people stand in small groups and begin to chat among themselves as the room empties.

Holding her reporter's notebook and a pen, she steps directly in front of Fuller, blocking his way, and asks politely, "Just one more question, if I might, Sheriff?"

He looks disgruntled but returns to the front. Again she waits for the lights, the sound and the camera to get ready before she speaks.

"Yes, ma'am?" he says, sighing as he picks up the table microphone and stands in front of where his deputies have retaken their seats.

The audience is seated again. The room becomes quiet.

"Sheriff Fuller, are you aware that one of the wolves' owners, Evie Ballard, is also missing and has been gone as long as the wolves? And that her husband's, that would be Mr. Ballard's first wife, died under mysterious circumstances?"

The crowd stirs with a collective, "Woooo!"

Fuller again, inhales, and frowns, his jaw tightening and his face beginning to flush. Cameras close in on him.

Duane, furious but trying to maintain his outward composure, crushes the sides of some papers he holds in his lap, out of sight of the cameras.

Fuller starts to answer and stutters a bit.

"Yes, er, we know she's missing, but we. um, think it is a domestic problem and not a criminal matter.

A rancher instantly raises his hand and stands, "Excuse, me, Sheriff. Could you elaborate?"

Fuller, now calmer, his face relaxed, says, "Ms. Ballard, the co-owner of the wolves, was reported missing the day the wolves escaped. Her vehicle was found on River Road, unlocked with the keys inside."

"What progress has been made in locating her?" Neil, the Bozeman reporter calls out, still seated.

Duane, unblinking, stares straight ahead. Again, under the table, he makes a fist.

Fuller, sounding very much the politician answers, "We suspect she's left the state. That's all I can tell you now."

Following up, Neil asks, "Then you've totally ruled out foul play?"

"We can't totally rule anything in or out until she's located. Please, no more questions at this time. We need to get this search underway, folks. We need to start right now. Got helicopters and search teams to coordinate."

He walks toward the door and the deputies stand to join him outside. As soon as he exits, Duane begins to whisper something confidentially to Fuller. They both glare at Laura. She and Destiny stop by her car where she retrieves several items and then heads for the barn.

Duane and Fuller flanked by other deputies, some in flight suits, use the hood of a patrol car to spread out a map. They point to an area and discuss their strategy. They each hold a mobile phone and a rifle, in addition to their handguns.

After a few minutes, Laura, on Solo, rides past them. She has rain gear tied to the saddle.

The officers all look up, then return to their planning. Destiny runs to Duane. He pets her briefly while ignoring Laura who avoids looking at him and rides on. Then Destiny runs to catch up with her.

When the deputies receive their instructions, they depart on some of the ranch's horses, riding in the direction of the loop trail where Laura has already gone. Other volunteers on the search team follow Jerry and the ranch staff on horseback in the loop's opposite direction. Everyone seems to be heading up toward the overnight-camping area.

84

False Alarm

Late in the day after the first search is over and the ranch atmosphere returns to somewhat normal, Vince, Fuller and Duane share a table in the back of the dining hall. All look tired, frustrated and worried.

Vince's cell phone rings and he grabs it from his front pocket, briefly grunts a reply and then hands the phone to Duane, saying, "For you. It's Linda Thornton at the D.A.'s office in Bozeman."

Duane, looking surprised, takes the call.

"Armstrong. Yes? Oh, okay. Fine. Guess it was worth checking. Thanks, Linda."

As he clicks off the phone, Duane seems relieved. He looks at Fuller and announces, "The bloody bone Keith found? Calf leg."

Fuller exhales loudly, looking relieved.

The three exit the building just as Jerry and some of the wranglers ride back in. They stop in front of the dining room where the CNN reporter interviews Laura on camera.

Duane avoids looking at her and skirts the entire area. He looks down and Destiny is again at his feet, her tail wagging. He walks away. Destiny sits down, cocks her head and looks puzzled.

Vince walks towards Jerry. The reporter abruptly ends Laura's interview and rushes over to Jerry.

Jerry and the wranglers dismount and place their rifles on the ground. A monitor near where the interview is taking place shows the CNN camera focusing first on the men, then a close-up on their rifles. The message is clear without a word said. If located, the wolves will be killed.

Someone pushes a microphone into Jerry's face and a reporter asks, "You men find anything up there? Locate the wolves? Kill any?"

"Nope!" Jerry snaps back. He is already weary and instantly becomes angry. He pushes the microphone aside, walks away.

85

Gathering Storm

Back in her cabin, Laura frantically collects a plastic tarp, binoculars, some snacks and a thermos. She grabs a camera and has her car keys in her hand when the phone rings. She picks it up.

"Yes?"

"Sis?"

"Hi, Ed. What's up?"

"You tell me! You were the one just interviewed on CNN! Live!"

Silence.

He continues, trying to sound calm but he's failing to pull it off, "So, tell me, Laura, just how you, who told us you were trying to get away, to disappear in fact, to heal, are suddenly in the middle of this major story on the network news?"

Ed sounds incredulous, adding, "What's wrong with this picture?"

"Long story short? I've just got to find out what's going on. I was with the wolf lady the day before she was reported missing. I can't, won't, give up on her."

Ed's tone changes. He becomes fatherly.

"Hey, girl. You're not even a working reporter anymore! Please give this up. For me? Please?"

She waits a few seconds, then sounds unconvincing as she brushes him off, "Fine. Fine. Gotta go."

She disconnects, not waiting to hear his reply.

Carrying all the items she gathered earlier, she dashes from the cabin, Destiny leading the way.

86

Back in the Saddle

Laura begins to prepare Solo for another ride.

Jerry stops by the barn and is surprised to see her. She ties a tarp and a raincoat behind the saddle and puts other items into saddle bags. He sees she's in a hurry.

"Goin' someplace?"

"Yep. Gonna ride up above the loop one more time before dark. I'm hoping for new discoveries."

Jerry scans the sky. "Looks like a storm's comin'. Rest of today's search may be called off 'til tomorrow. Want me to ride along?"

"Nope. Thanks. Get some rest. I'll be back in a few hours. I'll put Solo in his stall when I get back. No need to wait for us. Let's go, Destiny."

The dog complies and trots ahead of Solo on the trail.

Overhead, a news helicopter flies close to tree-top level, heading up into the hills, which again are fast becoming obscured by fog. The backdrop of clouds over some of the highest mountains also begins to look ominous in the fading sunlight. Within a few minutes, the helicopter turns back.

Upon reaching the area below the cave, Laura ties Solo and hikes up to the mouth of the cave again. When she's at the entrance, she hears wolves howling in the valley below.

Destiny suddenly takes off toward the howling.

Totally focused, Laura inches into the cave, searching the darkness with her flashlight. The pieces of bacon and sausage remain uneaten and are covered with ants and flies. No animals seem to have recently occupied the cave since she and the men saw it earlier.

Suddenly, she senses movement. She jumps, then freezes. "Hello?" she asks weakly, barely able to get out the word.

Straining to see into the dark, she shines her flashlight toward the back. There is no further movement, but she still feels something there. Shaking, she quickly heads for the faint light coming from the outside at the cave entrance. She gasps for breath and feels the walls closing in on her as she staggers outside.

87

New News

Keith has the television news on again in the back room when a woman customer comes in. He comes out to help her. She seems distraught.

"Know where Duane is? You won't believe it! Those damned wolves killed our sheep dog last night! I am gonna get to the bottom of this myself, if I have to."

"God, Eileen! How did it happened?" Keith says, genuinely concerned.

"John and I heard a commotion out in the yard and when we got there, we saw two big wolves. They were tearin' her apart. Killed her right in front of us! We screamed at them and they dropped her and left her there."

She begins to sob and dabs a tissue at her eyes, then picks up a carton of eggs and a loaf of bread, placing them near the check-out area. "We'd got her when she was just a puppy. Six years ago."

Keith shakes his head in empathy.

Looking especially sad, she adds, "We had a little burial service for her this morning and put her in the yard near the dog house."

"Sorry for ya," Keith says awkwardly.

The woman continues to blot her eyes and wipe tears from her face. "Can I use your phone to try to call Duane? Forgot mine in all of this!"

"Sure," he says, pointing to the house phone on the counter. "Duane's number for emergencies is written right there on the front of the phone."

As Keith scans her groceries, she looks back and declares with firmness, "These wolves have got to be stopped before they kill somebody!"

Keith bites his lip as if he knows something he can't reveal.

88

Caving In

There is only silence as Laura begins to force herself to return to the cave's opening. She does not turn on the flashlight at first. Stopping and backing away from the cave several times, she hesitates again and then finally moves forward, closes her eyes, and stops a few steps inside the cave. She feels the cooler temperature inside and suddenly her heart pounds wildly.

Her eyes fly open in horror. Unable to see anything in the pitch black, she feels herself back in the metal box. She is terrified, stiff. Unable to proceed and in a panic to escape the cave, she staggers back outside, shaking and gasping for breath, again.

Collapsing onto the ground, she realizes Destiny is nowhere in sight. "Destiny! Come here damn it, " she weakly calls out.

Destiny returns, struggling with a huge bloody bone which is covered with dirt. Laura sees the bone and shudders, thinking the worst. "No! Bad dog! Drop it!" she screams at Destiny.

Destiny first ignores her command and then drops the bone and starts backing away.

Within seconds, she begins to sneak back toward the bone, gets close, sniffs it and begins to lick it.

"No! Bad girl!" Laura, with more strength, yells.

Destiny immediately stops, sits.

Laura stands and approaches the bone cautiously. She examines it closely without touching it. She holds her hand over her mouth and nose to avoid the stench coming from it. Then, she spots a small piece of cow hide remaining on one portion, kicks it with her heavy boot, sending it back into the bushes. She backs away and sighs in relief.

Still shaking, she realizes it is impossible for her to re-enter the cave again, and she slowly walks back to where Solo is tied. She pats him, remounts and decides to double back and ride up the hill again toward Los Lobos Cabin. Passing the beaver pond, she, Solo and Destiny are strangely reflected through hazy shadows created by the almost-missing sun. Destiny races around and begins chasing her own unique shadow and barking at it.

In the distance, Laura sees horseback riders who have been part of the day's search team heading back downhill and across the valley. Dusk becomes afterglow. She decides to set up camp.

She removes Solo's saddle and covers it with a thick plastic bag, pulling it closed to seal the leather inside from the rain. She wouldn't want to explain to Vince how careless she had been with his property. Next, she replaces Solo's bridle with a hackamore she has carried tucked into her saddle bag. She loosely wraps its long rope to an aspen tree. He seems relieved to have the bit removed from his mouth and immediately bends his head down to hungrily eat grass.

Laura walks slowly up the hill and places the tarp on the ground overlooking Los Lobos Cabin. She takes out a thermos, her binoculars, and her camera. At first she uses the camera to focus on the cabin.

Destiny lies quietly beside her.

The weather starts to turn. Thunder rumbles in the distance. Through the binoculars, Laura sees Gregg walk out onto the porch, his long hair freely blowing in the gusty pre-storm wind. He checks some pet bowls near the stairs. He walks back inside and closes the door as rain starts to come down in big drops.

Laura gathers her things to leave when she suddenly hears movement, then footsteps behind her. She is frozen in place for several seconds before she hears Duane's voice.

"Duane? It's me. Don't shoot!"

"We won't. Jerry warned us you were coming up here!" he says, clearly annoyed. "We saw Solo tied down below and figured you were up to no good. Again!"

Duane appears with Mike, another deputy who is not thrilled to see her either. She frowns and puts the tarp over her head in tent-like fashion.

"Christ, Laura! What the hell are you doing? The search has been cancelled due to this rain. You planning to stay the night up here?"

She seems matter-of-fact with a little edge of nastiness, "I'm watching. I'm looking. Just like you."

Thunder rumbles again and a few more drops of rain start to fall. Wind whips the trees. Their voices rise to above-normal levels. The increasingly loud thunder makes Destiny uneasy. Laura pets her. Then she gestures to Duane and Mike to share the space under her tarp. They accept.

As he crawls under it, Duane says, "By the way, just for the record, Gregg never had to stand trial in his first wife's death. Ruled an accident. Two people have died in the exact same spot, exactly the same way."

"Don't care. I still feel Evie's in danger," she snaps back.

Duane says nothing more. The three sit in close quarters without speaking for a few minutes when they hear gunfire from Los Lobos Cabin. Using binoculars, they see Gregg out on his porch with his rifle raised in the their direction. He fires.

"Holy shit! Hit the deck!" Mike yells, scooting part way down the hillside away from the line of fire.

Laura, Duane and Destiny follow, leaving the tarp behind and sliding on the wet grass. They hug the ground. Bullets zing overhead. After several minutes, silence returns.

The rain has not developed but the sun is gone. Laura starts to wonder about Solo and leaves to check on him.

When she returns from securing him, dark clouds have created a night-like atmosphere. Mike and Duane have crawled back up to see if they can spot Gregg.

Gregg has turned on the porch light and he's down on all fours, creeping forward, rifle aimed, "Who's there? Who the fuck's out there?"

Before anyone answers, Gregg fires. Shots zing overhead again. Duane loads his rifle. Mike follows suit. Laura becomes alarmed. The men crawl forward on their bellies to assume combat position.

Duane shoves Laura out of the way. "Stay down, Laura! You're really out of your element. You should leave! Now!" He's not asking; he's ordering.

She complies, sliding down the slope and out of Gregg's line of fire.

Duane sees Gregg start back into the house when suddenly, several wolves trot toward him out of the wet blackness. He drops his rifle and greets them. They yip and jump with obvious delight. Gregg seems beside himself with glee.

Then, Solo whinnies, possibly seeing Laura approach.

Gregg grabs his rifle, turns, fires up the hill again. The wolves scatter.

"Police! Drop your weapon Gregg!" Duane shouts back.

Gregg fires again. Duane fires back. Gregg is hit. He falls.

Mike freezes, still focusing through his gun sight.

"Ohhhhhh!" Gregg moans. He lies half in and half out of the light from the porch.

Within a minute, the wolves slink back into the light, closer, closer. Their happiness has vanished and their mournful howls begin to echo through the mountains.

The largest wolf returns, slowly approaches to lick Gregg's face and then nudge him. Gregg remains motionless. Kusko lies down beside him and places his paw over Gregg's heart and his head on his chest.

Destiny is nowhere to be seen. Laura searches for her and becomes panicked due to the gunfire. Then, in the distance, what could be a faint human voice becomes barely audible.

"Sweet Destiny girl, you don't need to worry. I'm fine. I'm okay. Dear sweet thing. Where's mommy?"

Duane strains to locate the voice. Wolf cries drown it out. He concludes that Laura has located Destiny and is talking to her.

When Duane motions for Mike to hold his fire, Laura crawls back up to where Duane is lying and uses her binoculars to focus on the woods behind the cabin. She sees something move and she slips away again, jogging around the back of the cabin in the dark and drizzle to the wolf compound. She can see Gregg lying completely still nearby.

The wolves vanish.

Then Destiny cries out and runs at full speed past Gregg to Laura. She wags her tail, leaps up and licks Laura's face. Laura tries to pet and calm her but she will not stop moving.

Duane is frantic. He turns around to try to locate Laura, looks back at Gregg. He strains to focus through his gun sight. He can't determine if Gregg is badly wounded, unconscious or still armed and planning his next shot.

"Police! Drop your weapon, Mr. Ballard. We don't wanna hurt you anymore," Duane screams in dismay, adding, "Laura! Where the hell are you?"

Silence.

Duane and Mike inch down the hill toward the cabin, their guns aimed at Gregg. When they arrive beside him, they see his leg is bleeding heavily. His rifle lays a few feet from where he fell. The right leg of his jeans is soaked with blood. He appears to be semi-conscious. Mike retrieves Gregg's rifle and empties the ammunition.

Suddenly both Mike and Duane see Destiny dash down a path behind where Gregg lies. Laura follows her. The path is slippery and Laura stumbles as she makes her way through thick brush. Branches snag her clothing. She passes a gnarled, dead tree and falls.

Destiny runs directly toward what looks like an animal. It appears to be down on all fours negotiating in an odd crawling motion toward Laura.

The form comes to a stop and Destiny eagerly approaches, sniffing, whining. She puts her paw out.

Laura stops in her tracks. She tries to focus her eyes in the darkness, then hears a voice that sounds oddly soothing and is gently cooing, "Destiny, my Destiny."

Her own voice cracking, Laura says in a soft and broken tone, "It's okay Evie. You're okay. We didn't give up on you. You're safe now. You can come out. You're okay now."

Laura gains strength and walks forward. She places her hand on Evie's back, gently patting her like she would a dog. Her skin is cold, wet and crusted with dirt.

Evie slowly crawls forward on her hands and knees.

Duane and Mike watch as Laura emerges from the brush. First thinking it's one of the wolves alongside Laura and Destiny, the deputies merely step back with caution, assuming the animal is injured or weak but not dangerous.

Then Duane suddenly recognizes Evie, naked, filthy. Her hair is matted and her hands, feet and knees bloody from being scraped on the rocky ground. He does a double-take, putting down his rifle and immediately getting out his mobile phone.

Two more wolves appear, slowly following Evie as she approaches and lies down next to Gregg, placing her arm over his mid-section. She kisses his forehead. Gregg stirs. The wolves slowly slink into the background.

Laura approaches Evie and gently pulls her off Gregg to a standing position. She holds her.

Evie mumbles in Yupik, her head on Laura's shoulder.

Several more wolves come from the compound to investigate and gently brush up next to Evie, then Gregg, looking sad and curious. One begins to sniff Destiny who licks Evie's hand. Then, as if obeying a command, the wolves all return to the compound.

Mike kneels in the mud at Gregg's side, tying a tourniquet on his leg while Laura gently escorts Evie toward the cabin, taking off her own jacket and wrapping it around Evie's shaking body.

Duane takes a deep breath and begins to speak into the phone, "Search Unit One. Need a ambulance at Los Lobos Cabin. Gunshot victim needs immediate aid. They'll need paramedics and a four-by to get up here and a chopper to transport him from Big Timber. No, it's not an officer down. It's Gregg Ballard, the wolf owner. Leg wound. He's semi-consciousness."

"Also, better alert the medical team from county hospital, too. Have one for the mental ward also. Need to transport her. We have the ranch four- by parked on the other side of the hill from the cabin. Mike will meet you there; I'll stay with Ballard."

Laura, Evie and Destiny slowly enter Los Lobos Cabin. Low mournful howling emanates from the wolf compound.

The rain and clouds have cleared. Only stars and black sky surround the cabin.

89

Up in Smoke

Prior to meeting Duane at 5:30 as they agreed, Laura arrives at Crystal's at 5:15, knowing Duane is always exactly on time, not early, not late.

The parking lot is completely empty, except for one beat-up pickup with a large metal tool box across the back. Laura notices it, shrugs it off and for a split second realizes that seeing it has had no effect on her. It is just somebody's vehicle, somebody's toolbox, nothing more.

As she had hoped, no customers seem to be in the cafe. And, as usual at this time of the late afternoon, a column of gray smoke is puffing from the cafe's chimney. She can smell it as she gets out of her car.

Leaving Destiny inside for the moment, she opens the trunk and pulls out a large paper shopping bag with handles. Destiny whimpers, wanting to go with her, but as the door shuts, she quickly lies back down to wait for Laura's return.

Entering the front door, Laura notices the cafe's entire eating area is also empty and knows it's Crystal's routine to be back in the kitchen during pre-dinner hours, preparing for customers who usually show up between six and seven thirty.

Once inside, Laura walks to the back where a large pine log burns steadily in the small fireplace. She looks around to verify that Crystal is nowhere in sight, reaches into the bag and begins taking out the remaining contents of the infamous "box from hell" which she stuffed under her couch weeks ago. She planned to burn those items in the cabin fireplace, but with all that happened recently in the search for Evie, she never got around to it.

With no one watching or cheering her on, with no psychiatrist's words ringing in her ears and no college roommate instructing her, she slowly begins taking one item at a time, placing it on top of the burning log and pausing for a second or two to watch it consumed by flames.

As she releases each one, she feels lighter, freer and more in control of her life. The final piece is a small yellow Post-it note. On it are three handwritten words, "I forgive you."

The entire process takes less than three minutes. Valentine cards, vacation photos, newspaper articles about her being rescued and Al's subsequent trial are no longer part of her life. All the bad memories, too, have vanished.

One last item, the wedding album, feels heavy in her hand and in her heart. She places it firmly onto the log and it smothers the flames at first, almost causing the fire to go out completely.

Then small flames soon surround it. It too, is reduced to ash and smoke to be absorbed into the universe.

She returns to her car, opens the door and is greeted by a grateful Destiny who dashes to her feet, sits perfectly still and waits for what she knows is in Laura's pocket.

Destiny crunches the treat while Laura continues to stare at the smoke coming from the chimney.

Afterwards, she feels alone but not lonely.

90

Los Lobos Echoes

At exactly 5:35, Laura and Duane sit across from each other sipping coffee in the back booth. Destiny, the only dog ever allowed inside the cafe, lies at their feet.

Duane reaches down to pet her and smiles, "Hey, girl! My boss likes you a lot now! Still isn't too crazy about your mom, though."

Laura smiles at him with understanding.

It's crisp outside and both Laura and Duane leave their jackets on for a few minutes. He's brought along his ever-present yellow legal pad, pen attached, placing it on the seat beside him.

Laura seems completely at ease. She starts the conversation slowly. Her tone has lost any hint of sarcasm.

"So, let's see, you've got the wolves back in their pen and Gregg into the jail ward at the hospital?

"Yep. His doctor described his condition to me as sad, sober and sorry."

Laura sits forward, interested.

"Apparently, he asked for pen and paper and wrote an apology note to Evie, asking the doctor to take it to her. Doc said it had something odd written in there, asking her to forgive him and to please continue 'wolfing' with him, or something like that. The doc says they're both nuts, but he did say Gregg seemed truly sorry."

Laura smiles slightly at hearing the term *wolfing*, but doesn't think Duane is up for another lesson on Alaska vocabulary terms. Instead she asks, "And how's Evie?"

Duane takes a deep breath, holds his head in his hands and spills out, "On a Valium IV at County Hospital's psycho ward. Saw her there this morning. She's also in restraints, tied to the bed frame. Her eyes are vacant; her spirit is broken. When they brought her in, she told the medical staff she was single and lived in Akiak, Alaska, where she worked as a teacher."

As his words hit her, Laura's eyes shift from being filled with relief that the event is over to sudden sadness at Evie's obviously worsened mental state.

"Also her doctor said she had multiple scars and lots of other old injuries. Said Evie told him they were wolf bites and scratches, not revealing anything was done by Gregg. Said that was kinda typical though, not to reveal the real perpetrator. Doc said he wasn't sure what to believe after examining her x-rays since there were no broken bones."

Laura sighs, remembering she never revealed Al's violence toward her either.

"Just before I left, the Doc told me in a really serious tone, 'After all, they *are* wild animals!'" Duane adds.

Almost mumbling Laura says, "Did he mean Gregg or her wolves?"

Another deep sigh from Duane as he continues, "Thought I might get Evie to tell me what happened to her after she abandoned her Jeep. I wanted details for my report. We may never know if Gregg ever hurt her or not. But, when I tried to talk to her, she was in and out of speaking Yupik and she kept calling out for Brian."

At hearing the news, Laura says nothing, staring into her coffee cup.

"Her nurse told me privately that last night Evie had to be doped up to keep her from bothering other patients. Said she kept howling that eerie cry." Duane grimaces, then shudders.

"Poor Evie!" Laura says softly. "She didn't deserve this." She pauses and then asks, "You ever find the wolf pups?"

"Yep. Evie'd been living in the cave with them 'til the female was shot. They were way back in there all huddled together. They're fine, just hungry that's all."

Laura shakes her head.

Duane continues, "Problem now is what to do with them. We just locked them back in their enclosure. The other wolves seem to be attending to them. Neighbors are rotating taking food to the wolves, 'til Gregg gets back and the D.A. decides what to do. Probably all the charges will be dropped. Looks like his leg will heal quickly. Just a superficial wound."

Laura nods.

"Koehler lady's been on CNN all day. Wants the wolves taken back to Alaska and released. She wants animal rights people to donate to a fund she started to transport them back and release them into the wild."

Silence dominates for a couple of seconds as they both try to digest what has happened in less than 24 hours.

Then Laura, with a far-away look in her eyes, says, "This whole ordeal has taught me something."

Duane suddenly grins. His tone is mocking, authoritative, "Let me guess. Wolves can travel up to 40 miles a night?"

Laura, half-smiling, swats his hand.

Duane tries to be serious. "Sorry. Couldn't help myself. Go on, really. Sorry."

Laura chooses her words carefully and calmly as if, by saying them aloud, they become real for the first time. "Ya know how people often make incorrect conclusions totally opposite to the facts staring them in the face?"

He nods. "Yep. Like the old 'cry wolf' thing?"

"Yes. I actually saw what I realize now had to be Evie's footprints in that cave, alongside the other wolves' prints, but I ignored the blatant facts because I chose, maybe subconsciously, to continue to believe Gregg wanted her dead and buried, just like Al had wanted me dead."

"Guess maybe I'm guilty of that, too," he admits. "I pretty much believed Evie ran away with Brian, despite all the evidence that she hadn't. Still, I chose to believe all women are disloyal."

Laura looks deeply into his eyes and adds, "One more thing, too. I didn't see it in myself—only in Evie, but I learned that when you run away, you always take yourself with you."

Duane considers her words for a few seconds, smiles with sincerity and nods in agreement. Then he picks up his legal pad and flips to the place where he earlier wrote the six words on one page. He turns the pad sideways so Laura can read them. She recognizes them but looks puzzled.

"I learned something, too," he says. "I realized what life is all about and what's really important."

Laura re-reads the underlined words with new eyes, looks back into his and smiles broadly extending her hand across the table, slowly saying them aloud, "Loyalty, mate for life, family first."

He takes her hand in his and holds it gently.

Crystal, watching from the background, smiles at the couple.

Then Duane's tone changes. He takes back his hand, removes his jacket and sips some more coffee. Laura follows his lead.

"By the way, you and I were *both* wrong about what was in the big hole that Gregg dug.

Laura leans forward, looking intrigued.

"Oh?"

Duane seems to be enjoying slowly revealing bits of breaking news to the consummate reporter and doesn't quickly give away the bottom line, "Yep, you were so sure we'd find Evie's body down inside that hole, cold and stiff, and put there by her diabolical husband!"

Laura looks a bit sheepish and nods.

"And I was just as convinced we would only find wolf poop and the Ballard's recycled household garbage in there because I wanted, in the worst way, to believe that Evie'd just decided to abandon poor ol' Gregg for her ex-lover."

Laura becomes impatient, the reporter in her wanting the facts. She jerks on his hand to finish the story, "So, tell me, damn it!"

"But what Gregg really put in the hole were all their wedding photos, all her clothes, her books, the videos of her and Brian from Alaska, her favorite knick-knacks. It was every scrap of anything that reminded him of Evie. Even her old typewriter and some of the many fake letters she had written to herself, supposedly from Brian. Our deputies used Gregg's backhoe and dug everything up this morning and then sifted through it this afternoon."

Then he smiles, takes a breath and adds, "And you'll never guess what else he dumped in there!"

"What? Don't you dare keep me guessing!"

"The deputies found six full cases of beer, more than 50 uprooted marijuana plants, at least a kilo of dried pot and all his rolling papers and paraphernalia! Even his ashtray with the pot leaf on it was in there, broken in pieces."

Laura sighs. For the first time, she seems to realize she can relate on a personal level to Gregg's bizarre behavior, thinking about what she herself just burned in the restaurant fireplace.

The two sit quietly, digesting the details each has heard from the other.

The afternoon sun begins casting long shadows over the purple mountains. In silence, Duane and Laura hold hands across the table and stare through the picture window. In the distance, silhouetted, a colt and mare graze in the pasture. The always-short summer in the Crazies is coming to a close and autumn is approaching. Leaves on the aspen trees have already begun to change as Nature's cycle continues. The yellows and golds will become deep reds, and a stillness will soon set in as winter continues its inevitable advance.

Laura and Duane look into each other's eyes without speaking. Then, a knowing expression sweeps over her face.

"When I think about it, I guess Gregg only wanted to bury the past and his pain, right?"

Duane nods, "Yep. I guess we're all just looking for a happy ending."

He rises slightly from the booth's seat and leans forward across the table. She does the same. Their lips barely touch in a soft, tender kiss. Then they briefly put their foreheads together and sit back down, as Crystal shows up with a smile and the coffee pot.

The End

Epilogue

When the Bozeman newspaper arrives the following day and copies are placed into the news rack in front of Crystal's Cafe, the banner headline on the front page reads:

Lab Helps Solve Mystery of Missing Woman

The accompanying article's lead paragraph begins:
"Labs often play critical roles in helping solve unusual crimes by analyzing DNA evidence, fingerprints and other clues left at the scene. But one lab that actually located a woman missing for a week in the Crazy Mountains and helped solve the mystery of her whereabouts has four legs and is named Destiny."

Destiny's photo is next to the story.

About the Author

Julie Davey has loved the written word and school classrooms since she was four years old. Her late mother, Mozelle, used to tell anyone who would listen about how Julie, under five at the time, would sneak into the kindergarten class of the school next door to their Colorado Springs home, sit behind the "big" kids circled around the teacher, and wait for story time. In elementary school, when she wasn't riding her horse, riding her bike or hiking in Austin Bluffs near her house, she liked writing poems and stories.

Her first poem was printed in the Steele School newspaper when she was in third grade. Julie also wrote for her junior high school and high school newspapers and was editor of the Colorado Woman's College newspaper in Denver. She received her associate of arts degree in journalism from CWC, and her bachelor's degree in journalism and her master's degree in American Studies from California State University, Los Angeles.

She worked as a newspaper reporter and television writer in Laredo and as an investigative newspaper reporter in San Antonio, Texas, before moving to California where she became associate editor of *Engineering and Science Magazine* at the California Institute of Technology in Pasadena.

She taught journalism at Glendale High School and Fullerton College, where she also served as adviser for the campus newspapers. Under Julie's leadership, *The Hornet* at Fullerton College was awarded the Gold Crown in college journalism by Columbia University. She served as a writing consultant, working with the Yupik people in Alaska to write about their culture, lifestyles and traditions. Her story, *The Tale of Spirit Wolf* appears in a current Alaska public school textbook by Hoffman Educational, Inc.

Julie is the author of three other books: a political thriller, *La Caridad*; a non-fiction self-help book, *Writing for Wellness: A Prescription for Healing*; and a book of coincidences co-written with another Julie Ann Davey, an Australian author who shares the same name and many other life parallels, *"Coincidence or Something Else?"* All books can be purchased on Amazon.com and viewed on authorcentral.amazon.com

She and her husband live in Laguna Niguel, California. She spends her free time writing and volunteering at Camp Pendleton where she has taught, "Writing for Strength" to Marines returning from the Middle East, and Writing for Wellness at local hospitals and cancer centers, teaching patients how to write about their life experiences.

A two-time breast-cancer survivor, Julie has been recognized for her writing classes at City of Hope National Cancer Center and her resulting book. Honors include: the center's Heart of Hope Award; Humanitarian of the Year for the City of Duarte, California; Woman of the Week by CBS2 News in Los Angeles; and being named to the Colorado Springs Palmer High School Alumni Hall of Fame.

She treasures the written word and still feels most at home in a classroom.

Made in the USA
San Bernardino, CA
06 November 2017